CW01666476

BILLY BUDD

A tragedy based on the story by Herman Melville, of a fine young sailor persecuted by a malevolent master at arms on a British warship in 1798. When the latter falsely accuses Billy before the Captain, the youngster is unable to answer in his own defence because of a speech impediment, but is provoked into a blow which accidentally kills his accuser. The Captain, despite strong sympathy with Billy, which is shared by the whole crew, is obliged by the needs of naval discipline at a critical time, to sentence him to death.

THE HEREFORD PLAYS

General Editor: E. R. Wood

Maxwell Anderson
Winterset

Robert Ardrey
Thunder Rock

Robert Bolt
A Man for All Seasons
The Tiger and the Horse
Vivat! Vivat Regina!

Harold Brighouse
Hobson's Choice

Coxe and Chapman
Billy Budd

Gordon Daviot
Dickon

Barry England
Conduct Unbecoming

J. E. Flecker
Hassan

Ruth and Augustus Goetz
The Heiress

H. Granville-Barker
The Voysey Inheritance

(Ed.) E. Haddon
Three Dramatic Legends

Willis Hall
The Long and the Short and the Tall

Fritz Hochwälder
The Strong are Lonely

Henrik Ibsen
The Master Builder
An Enemy of the People

D. H. Lawrence
The Widowing of Mrs Holroyd and *The Daughter-in-Law*

Roger MacDougall
Escapade

Arthur Miller
The Crucible
Death of a Salesman
All My Sons

Bill Naughton
Spring and Port Wine

André Obey
Noah

J. B. Priestley
An Inspector Calls
Time and the Conways
When We are Married

James Saunders
Next Time I'll Sing to You
A Scent of Flowers

R. C. Sherriff
Journey's End

David Storey
In Celebration

J. M. Synge
The Playboy of the Western World and *Riders to the Sea*

Brandon Thomas
Charley's Aunt

Peter Ustinov
Romanoff and Juliet

John Whiting
Marching Song
Saint's Day
A Penny for a Song
The Devils

Oscar Wilde
The Importance of Being Earnest

Tennessee Williams
The Glass Menagerie

Louis O. Coxe and Robert Chapman

Billy Budd

BASED ON THE NOVEL BY HERMAN MELVILLE
with Authors' Introduction, Glossary and Notes

HEINEMANN EDUCATIONAL BOOKS
LONDON

Heinemann Educational Books Ltd

LONDON EDINBURGH MELBOURNE AUCKLAND TORONTO
SINGAPORE HONG KONG KUALA LUMPUR
IBADAN NAIROBI JOHANNESBURG
LUSAKA NEW DELHI

ISBN 0 435 22150 7

First published in the *Hereford Plays Series* 1966
Reprinted 1968, 1970 (twice), 1971, 1973, 1975

Published by
Heinemann Educational Books Ltd
48 Charles Street, London W1X 8AH
Printed and Bound in Great Britain by
Morrison and Gibb Ltd., London and Edinburgh

Contents

FOREWORD

Yea and Nay—
Each hath his say;
But God He keeps the middle way.

ALTHOUGH Herman Melville wrote those lines in another work, they apply to the terrible but fascinating sea tale of *Billy Budd.* Absolute good and absolute evil cannot live in this world together, according to Melville. Each must destroy the other, for human life is a compromise that follows the middle way.

Since Melville was a rejected and forgotten man when he wrote *Billy Budd* a few months before he died in 1891, no one thought much of his tale at the time. Even after it was published when Melville was beginning at last to interest the world, no one realized that *Billy Budd* contained the material for a remarkable play until Louis O. Coxe and Robert Chapman got to work on the manuscript a few years ago. The play was offered in the invitational series of the Experimental Theatre in 1949 under the cadaverous title of *Uniform of Flesh,* and it made an indelible impression on everyone who saw it.

As a theatre work, *Billy Budd* is exciting. For life on board a British warship in 1798 is full of colour and pageantry – the squalid life of the crew below decks, the grandeur of life among the afterguard, the austerity of discipline, the feuds between the men and officers, the interludes of wonder and calm at sea, the explosions of anger and treachery. During his seven years at sea, which ended in 1844, Melville served for fourteen months as sailor in an American warship, and he knew intimately the nature of the service.

Although his years at sea were the most fruitful of his life and he loved to look back on them, he was not an uncritical romantic, and he recognized shipboard life of that time as brutish, depraved and malevolent. Many writing hands have intervened between Melville's original manuscript and this trenchant play. But a theatregoer has an instinctive feeling that it has honestly caught the original spirit without romanticizing on the one hand or defaming on the other. There seems to be a basic truth under the power and viciousness of the life depicted in the play.

If *Billy Budd* were only a sea yarn, it would hardly have the distinction it brought to Broadway. But in the last interval of relative peace that concluded Melville's wretched life, he was thinking about the nature of what he had seen and felt throughout his crushing career. He had reached what Newton Arvin vividly describes as the 'perilous outpost of the sane' and had come back nearer the centre of human sympathy. There was much that he still did not understand. But he was convinced that absolute good and absolute evil must destroy each other; and, as Mr Arvin observes in his excellent critical biography, Melville rewrote the grand epic of the fall of man to communicate his conclusions.

Billy Budd is extraordinarily well done. In their dramatization Mr Coxe and Mr Chapman have never taken cheap advantage of a melodramatic plot. They have not underwritten or overwritten. They have not stacked the cards. Some of their play is written lightly in a vein of affable comedy. The tragic portions are written with taste, firmness and intelligence. Although *Billy Budd* is the dramatization of a novel, it is a fully wrought play in its own right. There is something translucent about both script and performance. Through them comes the earnest thought of a lonely old man who had been through hell and was beaten but not broken. He accepted the universal compromise but he never made it.

BROOKS ATKINSON

AUTHORS' INTRODUCTION

It is difficult now, in retrospect, to determine how and why we we arrived at a decision to make Melville's novel into a play. We had of course been familiar with the story for some time, and when in 1947 we actually began discussing the dramatic problems entailed in writing a play on the theme Melville gives us, we had only recently been very close to the novel. Perhaps the 'Melville Revival' influenced us; it may have been the desire to find a theme and action that was inherently poetic and non-realistic. Above all, one idea or purpose seems clear; that we saw in *Billy Budd* a morality play.

History and the literature of the past serve many functions for the present. Men like to think that they look at the past and its works objectively, with an evaluating eye, yet most of us know that any age seeks from the past justifications and flatteries; looks for ideas in a literature of another time and selects from them those that seem particularly pertinent to the seeker, whether the ideas found be actually *there* or not. Writers and critics have a way of reviving the dead with the purpose of forcing them to say certain things we wish they had said, or to reaffirm what they perhaps did say, though too often in accents and in a tone to which we do violence in our translation. But this is no evil, and surely it is a mark of greatness in a writer if his accents and tone are various enough to command the languages of various times and places. For us, as inchoate playwrights, in January of 1947, Melville's story of good, evil, and the way the world takes such absolutes was material enough for two veterans of a war, a depression, and the moving cold front.

Today morality is not popular; perhaps it has never really been so. In our day it is popularly lamented and celebrated in absentia, much modern criticism being devoted to the discovery of morality in the least likely places. Yet to find the stuff of dramatic morality pure is no easy task, since, however hard one may try, Freud will turn up and all one's efforts will post off to the clinic and the analyst's couch to work out there a modern salvation. Thus a critic can say of our play that such a phenomenon as Claggart could never appear in our world with all we know of the psyche and the ego. We doubt that. We are certain that neither a Billy nor a Claggart ever was or could be, and, to undercut a little ground, we add that the same is true of an Oedipus. But all these personae are true as symbols, representing as they do certain permanent attitudes, qualities, moral images. It is just this figuring forth that Melville's novel so pre-eminently effects for our time, and if we do indeed lament a lack of standards for this age we can at least see in *Billy Budd* the potentiality of a new vision, a vision that allows a man to think generally about absolutes without feeling he is violating 'truth' because he has not polled a sample of his generation to get the 'facts'. The trouble is, Melville has stated a fact but it is not the kind of fact men either like or know what to do with.

Perhaps all this has less to do than we think with how our play got written or even started. Once that start was made, however, we found ourselves bound by the novel, and it was only after some experimentation that we realized how little Melville had given us that was theatrical or, perhaps, finished. There was certainly little reason why he should; the drama is surely in the novel, but it is an inner, imagined drama. Our job was to put it on a stage and give flesh to the finely articulated skeleton – no small task in view of the deceptive nature of the novel. What seems to the casual reader mere padding in *Billy Budd* (the novel) is vital information – about the great mutinies, the Napoleonic Wars, the British Navy, the moral and social climate. And Melville was assuming an audience of some culture (if at this stage he was able to assume an audience at all) which would know about the Rights of Man, the Terror, Rodney, and what manner of man Captain Vere is intended to represent. All this we had to show, to bring to life and to give to the audience in such a way that the information might not arrive as information but as an ambience. We do not say that we have done this, only that it must be done if there is to be a real play. This is a morality play and we do not apologize for its being such.

LOUIS O. COXE
ROBERT CHAPMAN

CHARACTERS

EDWARD FAIRFAX VERE, *Captain, Royal Navy*
PHILIP MICHAEL SEYMOUR, *First Officer*
JOHN RATCLIFFE, *First Lieutenant*
BORDMAN WYATT, *Sailing Master*
GARDINER, *a Midshipman*
REA, *a Midshipman*
SURGEON
JOHN CLAGGART, *Master-at-Arms*
SQUEAK, *Master-at-Arms' man*
THE DANSKER, *Mainmast man*
JENKINS, *Captain of the Maintop*
PAYNE, *Maintopman*
KINCAID, *Maintopman*
O'DANIEL, *Maintopman*
BUTLER, *Maintopman*
TALBOT, *Mizzentopman*
JACKSON, *Maintopman*
BILLY BUDD, *Foretopman*
HALLAM, *a Marine*
MESSBOY
STOLL, *Helmsman*
DUNCAN, *Mate of the Main Deck*
BYREN, *Relief Helmsman*
DRUMMER
OTHER SAILORS, *crew of the* INDOMITABLE

The entire action takes place aboard H.M.S. *Indomitable* at sea, August 1798, the year following the Naval mutinies at Spithead and the Nore.

ACT ONE

SCENE I

Although outside it is a fine morning in early August, the between-decks compartment of the crew's quarters assigned to the maintopmen is dark and shadowy except for the light spilling down the companionway from above and, through the open gun-ports, the flicker of sunlight reflected on the water. The smoking-lamp burns feebly over a wooden mess table and two benches lowered for use.

JENKINS *sits at the table mending a piece of clothing. In the shadow* THE DANSKER *sits motionless on a low sea chest, smoking a pipe. Neither man speaks for a long minute.*

Then JACKSON *appears on deck at the top of the companionway and lurches down into the compartment. He is doubled up in pain.*

CLAGGART (*off*): You there! Jackson!

JACKSON: God, he's followed me!

JENKINS: Who?

JACKSON: Master-at-Arms. He'll send me aloft again sure, and I can't hang on . . .

JENKINS: What the devil's wrong with you, Jack? Here, sit down.

CLAGGART (*entering down the companionway*): Why have you come down off the mainmast, Jackson? Your watch over?

JACKSON: Sick, Mister Claggart, I'm so sick, I was shaking up there on the yard till I near fell off.

JENKINS: Grab an arm, mate, I'll take you along to sick-bay.

CLAGGART: Stand away from him, Jenkins. (*To* JACKSON.) Just where does this sickness strike you, in the guts, or limbs? Or in the head? Does it exist at all?

JENKINS: You can see he's sick as a puking cat, plain as your stick.

CLAGGART: The role of Good Samaritan hardly fits you, Jenkins. (*To* JACKSON.) Now up, man. Turn topside.

JACKSON: I can't, I can't, I'm deathly sick, God help me, sir!

CLAGGART: That's hard. But this ship needs all hands. We're undermanned. The aches and pains of landsmen have their cures, but ours have none. You'll have to get aloft. Now move!

JACKSON: I ain't bluffing, sir, I swear I'm not! Please, Mister Claggart . . . I got Cooper's leave, he says all right, I can come down.

CLAGGART: You have not got my leave. Cooper is captain of the maintop and ought to know better. Four men to every spar, and no replacements. Now up. Back where you belong.

JACKSON (*starts up the ladder*): God, sir, I can't, I can't stand it! It'll be my death, sure!

CLAGGART: No more talk, man! Up you get! Start! (JACKSON *goes painfully up the ladder and out of sight on deck.* CLAGGART *starts out after him.*)

JENKINS (*mutters*): God damn you!

CLAGGART: Did you say something, Jenkins? (*Jenkins does not answer.* CLAGGART *goes out, calling after Jackson.*) Now Jackson, get along. Up! Up!

JENKINS: I'll stick him one day before long! I will, if I hang for it.

Laughter and talk in the next compartment followed by entrance of BUTLER, TALBOT *and* KINCAID.

BUTLER: Messboy!

TALBOT: Haul in the slops!

KINCAID: Suppose we'll get the new man? The jack they 'pressed this morning off that merchantman? I see 'em come alongside just now.

TALBOT: I pity that poor bloke, so I do. I hear they get good pay on merchant ships. Eat good, too, and then treated like the goddam Prince of Wales. (MESSBOY *enters with an iron pot of food and spits on the deck.*) Spit in it, damn you. Can't taste no worse.

MESSBOY: Ain't nobody making you eat it, mate. You can wash your feet in it if you like. (O'DANIEL *and* PAYNE *enter.*)

TALBOT: What's eating you, Jenkins? Ain't you going to join the banquet?

JENKINS: By God, I seen a thing just now I won't stand for! I'm sitting here off watch, and I seen it all. That blacksnake Claggart kicked Jackson back aloft, and him sick as a baby in a cradle, as any fool could see.

PAYNE: He's the Master-at-Arms, ain't he?

JENKINS: Cooper sent him down. Who's captain of the starboard watch, him or Claggart? Cooper could have found him a relief. Plain murder, by God!

TALBOT: You think Claggart can get away with what he does without Captain Starry Vere knows what's going on? Him and that red snapper Seymour, and them other officers!

JENKINS: Jackson'll fall. By God, no man can hang to a spar sick like that. He'll fall sure.

O'DANIEL: Tush, man, nobody falls in His Majesty's Navy. We lose our footing. 'Tis flying we do, to be sure.

TALBOT: I tell you it's Vere that's the cause of it! Our glorious fine Captain Vere, with a league of braid around his arm and a straight back!

O'DANIEL: Vere, is it. As captains go, mate, let me tell you, he's an angel with a harp alongside of the skipper on the *Royal George*. Every day that one flogged a dozen men. Picked 'em by lottery, by God. Never took the gratings down till they was rusty with blood. Ho! This Vere's a saint in heaven after him.

JENKINS: Ram the *Royal George* and everybody in her!

Claggart's the man we want, and the sooner the better, say I!

O'DANIEL: Ah, we'd 'ave had him puking his blood at Spithead, the devil rot him.

BUTLER: You was there, O'Daniel? At Spithead?

O'DANIEL: Aye. I was. Wherever you do find Englishmen doing a smart thing, you'll find an Irishman is at the bottom of it. Oho, fine it was, every day of it, with the officers quaking in their cabins, spitting green, and the whole English government wetting their breeches from the fear of us! Ah, lovely it was, lovely!

TALBOT: Belay your Irish noise, you fat-mouthed mackerel-snatcher. I'll tell you this, we need men on here is not afraid to use their knives if it come to that. And you can be sure it will come to that, mind my word, Mickey Cork.

JENKINS: What did you ever use your knife for, Talbot, but to scratch your lice? Ah, you're a dancing daredevil, you are for sure.

TALBOT: I'll be happy to show you, if you like.

JENKINS: Trouble will be hunting you out, mate, if you're not careful.

TALBOT: Trouble! You whoreson cockney cullion! There's not a man aboard don't know you for a coward, you whining bitch-boy!

JENKINS: Get out.

TALBOT: Damn you, I'm not afraid of you, or your snivelling hangbys, either!

JENKINS: Move! Get out of it, or by God I'll run my knife to the hilts in you!

TALBOT: You son of a whore! Pigsticker!

They attack one another with drawn knives, JENKINS *reaching suddenly across the table to seize Talbot. Silently they thrash around the compartment upsetting benches and food while the others look on unmoved.*

O'DANIEL: Ah, I do love to see two Englishmen fighting each

other. It's fonder they are of killing themselves than fighting their proper foes. (*Laughs hoarsely.*)

PAYNE: Tomorrow's rum on Jenkins. Any bets?

KINCAID: He never lost one yet.

JENKINS *throws Talbot on the deck and holds the knife at his throat for a moment before letting him up, first taking his knife. He holds out his hand.*

JENKINS: I'm leading seaman in this compartment, mind that. (TALBOT *hits Jenkins' hand and goes off angrily.*)

KINCAID: You're captain, that's all right by me.

O'DANIEL: Eyes in the boat, lads. Here comes *pfft*-face.

SQUEAK, BILLY *and* GARDINER *appear on deck and start down the companionway.*

GARDINER: Hang it, step lively, boy! Your ship is . . . Doff your hat to officers when they speak to you! By God, I'll teach you to touch your hat to a midshipman's coat, if it's only stuck on a broomstick to dry!

BILLY: Aye, sir. (*The men react to Gardiner with yawns and gestures behind his back.*)

GARDINER: Very well. Your ship is H.M.S. *Indomitable* now, and we sail her tautly, and we tolerate no nonsense. Is that clear?

BILLY: Aye, sir.

GARDINER (*to Squeak*): See this new man is assigned to a watch, and get him squared away. (*To Billy.*) You're green, of course, I can see that. But I expect we'll ripen you. (*He trips going up the ladder and* SQUEAK *tries to help him.*) Carry on. (GARDINER *exits.*)

SQUEAK: My name's Squeak. I'm the Master-at-Arms' man. Have you met the Master-at-Arms yet, Mister Claggart? (BILLY *shakes his head.*) Oh, you'll like him. He's a nice fellow. (O'DANIEL *chokes on his pipe smoke and the other men react similarly.*) Stow your gear along in there. This here's the larboard section of the maintop. Captain of the watch is

Jenkins. Him, there. Report to him. (*He pats Billy on the chest and grins before starting up the ladder.*)

JENKINS: What's a green hand dumped in here for?

SQUEAK: Complaining, Jenkins?

JENKINS: I'm asking. What's wrong with that?

SQUEAK: Mister Claggart wants him here, that's why. Maybe he wants for Billy Boy to set you pigs an example. Refer any more complaints to the Master-at-Arms! (*Exits.* BILLY *grins at the men, who return his look.*)

BILLY: My name is Budd. Billy, if you like.

KINCAID: I'm Kincaid. This is where you swing your hammock. That's O'Daniel, this here's Payne, and Butler. This is Jenkins, captain of the watch, and that old jack's called the Dansker. Don't know why, unless maybe he's Danish. You never had a real name, Dansker?

THE DANSKER: Not for many years.

BUTLER: You'd be the new impressed man?

BILLY: Aye, so I am. I just came off the *Rights of Man* this morning.

THE DANSKER: Forget about the *Rights of Man* now, lad.

JENKINS: How long you been going to sea, baby?

BILLY: About ten years, but in the merchant service.

O'DANIEL: Merchant service! Whissht! (*Laughs hoarsely.*)

BILLY: I know I'm new at Navy work, and probably there'll be some things I'll need help with.

JENKINS: No doubt, little boy.

BILLY: I'll learn fast, never fear. But she's a big old girl, this ship. I never was in a ship-of-the-line before. I'd have got lost trying to find the mess by myself. Maybe fallen in the magazine!

O'DANIEL: Ah, you get used to it. She's big, is this tub, but she's not so big you can get lost in her.

PAYNE: Sometimes I wish to God you could. Maybe we could lose O'Daniel. (BILLY *laughs and the others join.*)

BILLY: You're Irish, aren't you? I like the Irish. There was an Irishman on the *Rights of Man*, with big red whiskers . . . when I came away, he gave me a silver knife. This is it.

O'DANIEL: It's a beauty. Mind you keep an eye on it.

BUTLER: What's the matter, boy?

BILLY: I was just thinking, maybe I won't ever see my friends again.

O'DANIEL: If they was Irish, don't you worry at all. The Irish is liable to turn up almost anywheres, excepting England and the fires of hell, which is much the same.

PAYNE: Danny, if it wasn't for the harps, the devil wouldn't have nothing to do. What was potato-eaters doing on a merchant ship?

BILLY: Just sailors, like me. Most of us had no other home, even the skipper. He was a kind old bloke. Looked fierce, but he always had a kind word. Used to keep a bird in a cage in his cabin. The skipper let me feed the bird sometimes. Worms right out of the ship's biscuit. That was mostly all the meat we got.

O'DANIEL: The bargemen in a Navy biscuit would eat the bird.

KINCAID: Sit down here, Bill. Maggots or not, this is what we get. You hungry?

BILLY: I'm always hungry.

KINCAID: Try your first sample of His Majesty's bounty. We don't know what it is, but we been eating it for a long time.

BUTLER: Here, eat mine. Tastes like it's been eat before, anyhow.

JENKINS: Give him more lobscouse, Butler. We got to keep the roses in his cheeks, ain't we, boy?

BILLY (*laughing*): I could eat anything right now. Even this.

O'DANIEL: Help you to forget about home and mother, lad.

JENKINS: Tell us about home and mother, Baby Budd.

BILLY: There's not much to tell. I've got no home, and never had a family to remember.

JENKINS: Ain't that too bad.

BILLY: Oh, I'd feel a lot worse if I'd been 'pressed with a wife and children.

KINCAID: That's the truth.

O'DANIEL: We're all patriotic volunteers.

KINCAID: Guano! Wait till my hitch is up, you won't see no more of me.

BUTLER: Three weeks drunk in Portsmouth, then back in the ruddy fleet.

THE DANSKER: Men like us got no other home.

O'DANIEL: No other home, is it? Ah 'tis so thick the sweet thoughts is in here, I can scarce breathe.

PAYNE: Then you can strangle or get out.

JENKINS: Aye, get along, you lousy harp, give us some fresh air.

O'DANIEL: If you begged me to stay itself, I'd be off to where there's smarter lads. Boy, let you pay no heed to these white mice, mind what I say. And be hanged, the lot of yous! (*He starts up the ladder.*)

KINCAID: You'll catch it, Danny, if Captain holds an inspection.

O'DANIEL (*returning*): Ah whissht, I was forgetting that. And I do think that me figure shows up better here below than it does in the broad daylight.

BILLY: Inspection today?

PAYNE: Ah, the Old Man crawls over the ship any time he ain't got nothing else to do. You never know when till you see him.

KINCAID: What the devil he wants to inspect this hooker for, I can't figure. He's seen it before.

BUTLER: He ain't seen Billy.

BILLY: What's the Captain like? On the *Rights of Man*, the captain . . .

JENKINS: You going to jaw some more about that rocking horse? I suppose *you* was at Spithead, too?

BILLY: Spithead? Where is that?

JENKINS: A little party the Navy had a year ago. A mutiny, Baby, a mutiny. Know what that is?

BILLY: Why did they mutiny?

O'DANIEL: Arra, it's easy to see you're new to the Navy.

JENKINS: Jimmy-Legs is ten good goddam reasons for it, himself.

BILLY: Who's Jimmy-Legs?

KINCAID: Master-at-Arms. We call him Jimmy-Legs.

BUTLER: Watch out for that one, Billy.

PAYNE: He's the devil himself between decks.

O'DANIEL: What d'you expect, the saints of heaven? Not in an English tub.

BILLY: Why don't you like the Master-at-Arms?

JENKINS: You'll find out soon enough, Baby.

BUTLER: Watch him, boy. Jenkins can tell you. He's had a time or two with Claggart.

JENKINS: Aye, and I'll have another, one day before too long.

BUTLER: Sure, Jenkins. You look after Bill.

JENKINS: How old are you, kid? Sixteen?

BILLY: I don't know, maybe . . . twenty.

JENKINS: He don't even know how old he is! My guess is, too young to know what his parts are for.

O'DANIEL: Is it anybody is that young?

KINCAID: Stow it, Jenkins. Come on, don't pay no attention to him. He's feeling ugly today.

JENKINS: Well now, ain't you getting holier than a goddam bishop. Let him talk up for himself, if he don't like it.

KINCAID: Stow it, I say. You got no reason to crawl over Bill. Let him be.

BILLY: That's all right, Tom. I don't mind a joke. Black's the white of me eye, mates! (*All laugh except Jenkins.*)

JENKINS: Mama taught you pretty manners, huh? Oh! Ain't got no mama, you say? Well now, think what that makes you! (*Laughs.*)

BILLY: Tell me what you mean, Mister Jenkins.

PAYNE: What's gnawing you, Jenkins? Can't you see the boy's trying to be friendly?

JENKINS: You forgetting who's leading seaman here? Come on, Baby, talk back, why don't you? Scared?

BILLY: N-no. Why do you think I'd be scared, M-M-Mister Jenkins?

JENKINS: He stammers! What do you know! The little bastard's so scared he's stammering.

BILLY: Don't call me that again.

JENKINS: Sounds good, ha? Sounds fine. I like the way it rolls out your mouth. Bastard Baby Budd . . .

BILLY *strikes him.* JENKINS *staggers and falls, pulls a knife and gets up, lunging at Billy.* PAYNE, BUTLER *and* KINCAID *get up and stand close to Billy, silently protecting him.*

JENKINS: Get away, God damn you! He's got to find out who gives orders here.

KINCAID: Not this time, Jenkins. Lay off.

O'DANIEL: Belay it. You're wearing me out, the pair of yous.

BUTLER: Put away the knife. (JENKINS *sees their determination and relaxes a little, uncertain what to do.*)

BILLY: Will you shake hands? Or would you rather fight?

JENKINS: You little bas . . . (*Lunges forward.* BILLY *catches his arm and bends it, holding Jenkins cursing and powerless.*)

BILLY: That's enough, mate. Pipe down and let us be.

O'DANIEL: Good lad! Save the great strength is in you, Jenkins, for fighting the devil is after your soul.

JENKINS: All right, all right. You can let me go now.

O'DANIEL: Leave him go, lad. I won't hurt him at all.

BILLY: You're like Red Whiskers on the *Rights*, he liked to fight too. (*Freeing him.*) Will you shake hands, mate?

JENKINS (*momentarily uncertain what to do*): Shake hands, is it? . . . Well, you beat me fair. You got guts, which is more than I give you credit for. (*They shake hands.*)

KINCAID: You're a hell of a peacemaker, Bill.

PAYNE: That's the only time I ever hear Jenkins eating his own words.

O'DANIEL: Ah, that's a terrible diet, would make any man puke.

JENKINS: Don't you be getting any wrong ideas. I'm still a match for you!

KINCAID: Better belay your mess gear, Bill.

JENKINS: Where you come from, Baby?

PAYNE: Stow it! Jimmy-Legs! (BILLY *goes on talking as* CLAGGART *enters.*)

BILLY: I don't know, I guess from Portsmouth. I never lived ashore, that I can remember. Where do you come from? (*Drops a pot on deck.* CLAGGART *stands over him.*)

CLAGGART: Handsomely done, young fellow, handsomely done. And handsome is as handsome did it, too. You can wipe that up, Jenkins. (*To* BILLY.) What is your name?

BILLY: Budd, sir. William Budd, ship *Rights of Man*.

CLAGGART: Your ship is H.M.S. *Indomitable* now.

BILLY: Aye, sir.

CLAGGART: You look sturdy. What was your station aboard the merchantman?

BILLY: M-m-mizzentopman, sir.

CLAGGART: You like that station?

BILLY: Aye, sir, well enough.

CLAGGART: How long have you been at sea?

BILLY: Ten years, sir, near as I can tell.

CLAGGART: Education?

BILLY: None, sir.

CLAGGART: So. You come aboard with nothing but your face to recommend you. Well, while beauty is always welcome, that alone may not avail us much against the French. There are other requirements in the service.

BILLY: I'll learn quickly, sir.

CLAGGART: The sea's a taskmaster, young fellow. It salts the sweetness out of boyish faces. You cannot tell what motion lies asleep in that flat water. Down where the manta drifts, and the shark and ray, storms wait for a wind while all the surface dazzles.

BILLY: I am a seaman, sir. I love the sea. I've hardly lived ashore.

CLAGGART: Then let the wind and sea have licence to plunder at their will. As of today, a new maintopman swings between sky and water. (*He turns toward the ladder and notices the mess on deck.*) I thought I asked you to wipe that up, Jenkins.

JENKINS: That's the messboy's job.

CLAGGART: Clean up, Jenkins. (JENKINS *hesitates.*) That is an order. Turn to.

BILLY: I'll give you a hand, Jenkins. Come on.

CLAGGART: Ah, there. See how helpful Billy is. Why can't you take a leaf from this innocent young David's book, Jenkins? (*Turns away.* JENKINS *accidentally brushes against him and receives a savage cut from Claggart's rattan across his face.*) Watch what you're doing, man!

JENKINS: I swear . . .!

CLAGGART: Yes, what is it that you swear? Well, speak. Nothing at all to say? Then hear me: I have my methods with unruly tempers.

On deck there is a loud crescendo scream and a crash. Running footsteps, shouts, voice calling for the Surgeon. The men surge toward the ladder.

CLAGGART: Stand fast! (SQUEAK *enters down the hatchway,*

whispers to Claggart.) All right, I know. (SQUEAK *comes down into the compartment and runs off.)*

JENKINS: It's Jackson! I knew it, by God, I told you so!

Men turn to stare at Claggart as several sailors enter down the companionway, bearing the body of Jackson, inert and shattered. They carry him through the compartment and off to sick-bay.

SURGEON *(as he moves through the compartment)*: Clear the way, you men. Take him into the sick-bay, through here. Carry him gently. Easy, now. Easy. *(Exit.)*

JENKINS *(pointing to Claggart)*: He sent him back aloft. Killed him, he did!

O'DANIEL: Might as well have knifed him.

CLAGGART: Stand fast. Stop where you are. Your man Jackson is looked after.

O'DANIEL *(in a low voice)*: Then he's a dead man surely.

CLAGGART: Who spoke?

JENKINS: We'll have a showdown now! After him, mates! Cut into him!

The men move toward Claggart in a rush, drawing knives and cursing him, as CAPTAIN VERE *appears in the companion hatchway.*

VERE: Stand fast! Hold where you are. Master-at-Arms, what is the matter here? *(The men stop in their tracks and stare at* VERE, *who comes part way down the ladder.)*

CLAGGART: These dogs are out of temper, sir.

VERE *(to men)*: You will come to attention when I address you! Let me remind you that this ship is at war. This is a wartime cruise, and this vessel sails under the Articles of War. Volunteer or 'pressed man, veteran seaman or recruit, you are no longer citizens, but sailors: a crew that I shall work into a weapon. One lawless act, one spurt of rebel temper from any man in this ship, high or low, I will pay out in coin you know of. You have but two duties: to fight and to obey, and I will bend each contumacious spirit, each stiff-necked prideful soul of you, or crush the spirit in you if I must. Abide by the Articles of War and my commands, or they will cut you down. Now: choose. (*The men are silent.*) Very well. Master-at-Arms, this accident on deck, the sailor fallen from the yardarm. Do you know how it occurred?

CLAGGART: I do not, sir.

VERE: You are his messmates. Does any man of you know how this occurred? (*To Butler.*) You?

BUTLER: No, sir.

VERE: Jenkins, do you?

JENKINS (*hesitates a moment.* CLAGGART *moves slightly, tapping his hand with the rattan*): No, sir.

VERE (*notices the cut on Jenkins' face*): What's this, what's this? Speak up, man. I want no random bloodshed aboard this ship.

JENKINS: I . . . fell, Captain. Fell, and . . . and cut my cheek.

VERE: I see. You fell. Master-at-Arms, you will excuse this man from duty till the Surgeon tends him.

CLAGGART: Aye, aye, sir.

VERE: We must not wound ourselves, draining the blood from enterprise that takes a whole man. (*He turns to go up the ladder and sees Billy.*) Well. This is a new face. Who are you, boy?

CLAGGART: Maintopman 'pressed from the *Rights of Man* this morning, sir. William Budd.

VERE: Let him speak for himself. (BILLY *tries to speak but can only stammer incoherently.*) That's all right, boy, take your time. No need to be nervous.

BILLY: I saw a man go aloft, sir, as I came on board just a while ago. He looked sick, sir, he did. This officer was there, too, he can tell you. (*To Claggart.*) Don't you remember, sir?

VERE: Did you send a sick man aloft, Master-at-Arms?

CLAGGART: I did not, sir.

VERE: Very well. (*To Billy.*) Well, Budd, I hope you take to Navy life and duty without too much regret. We go to fight the French and shall need wits and hearts about us equal to the task.

BILLY: I'll do my best, sir.

VERE: I'm sure you will. We are all here to do our several duties, and though they may seem petty from one aspect, still they must all be done. The Admiral himself looks small and idle to the man like you who can see him from the maintop, threading his pattern on the quarterdeck. The Navy's only life. (SURGEON *enters.*)

SURGEON: Captain – Jackson, the man who fell just now – he's dead, sir.

VERE (*after a pause*): Carry on, Master-at-Arms. (*He goes out up the companionway.* SURGEON *exits.*)

CLAGGART: You've made a good impression on the Captain, Billy Budd. You have a pleasant way with you. If you wish to make a good impression on me, you will need to curb your tongue. Jenkins, I thought you were ordered to sick-bay. Jump to it. And I suggest you change that shirt. See how fouled it is with a peculiar stain. Why can't you keep clean like Billy here? (*He strikes Jenkins viciously on the arm with his rattan, smiles at him, and exits up the ladder.*)

JENKINS: God damn his flaming soul! I can't stand it no more!

BILLY: I don't see what you can do, mate. He didn't mean it when he hurt you then.

JENKINS: Listen boy, I know Jimmy-Legs. He lives on hurting people. Stay away from him, and keep your mouth shut, if you don't want trouble.

O'DANIEL: Did you hear the lad speak up to the skipper?

PAYNE: Aye, you watch your tongue, Bill. Claggart will be after you for talking up like that.

KINCAID: He's a cool one, Billy is. None of us got the nerve.

BUTLER: It's nerve gets a man in trouble in this tub.

THE DANSKER: Jimmy-Legs is down on you already, Billy.

BILLY: Down on me? Why, he's friendly to me.

JENKINS: Claggart don't make no friends.

O'DANIEL: You seen Jackson when they brought him below. That's how friendly he gets. (*Bosun's pipe off.*)

DUNCAN (*off*): Relieve the watch!

KINCAID: First watch on the *Indomitable*, Bill. Better lay up to the mainmast and report. (*Exit.*)

BUTLER: Don't slip off the yardarm.

PAYNE: Watch your step.

BILLY: Not me. You watch for me. Got to find the mainmast, and I'm in a hurry.

O'DANIEL: You'll never find your way in this old tub. I'll come along and show you. If anybody comes calling for O'Daniel while I'm out, take the message.

PAYNE: O'Daniel couldn't find his breeches if they wasn't buttoned on. You come with me. (BILLY *and* PAYNE *go off.*)

JENKINS: Poor bastard. I pity him, I do.

BUTLER: He's dead, ain't he? Better off than us.

JENKINS: Not Jackson. I mean the baby here. Billy.

BUTLER: We could have fared worse for a messmate.

JENKINS: Aye. He can take care of himself. Heave up the table.

SCENE 2

In the early evening of the same day, the off-duty sections of the crew are mustered aft on the maindeck for Jackson's funeral. Above them CAPTAIN VERE *stands uncovered at the forward break of the quarterdeck, reading the Committal Prayer. The westward sky is bright yellow and red, but fades into darkness as the scene progresses.*

The men are uncovered and stand at attention.

VERE: Unto Almighty God we commend the soul of our brother departed and we commit his body to the deep, in sure and certain hope of the resurrection unto Eternal Life, through our Lord Jesus Christ, at whose coming in glorious majesty to judge the world, the sea shall give up her dead, and the corruptible bodies of those who sleep in Him shall be changed and made like unto His glorious body according to the mighty working whereby He is able to subdue all things unto Himself. Amen.

MEN: Amen.

Short drum-roll followed by a muffled splash as Jackson's body slips over the side. Then the bosun's pipe. Officers cover and march off.

CLAGGART: Ship's company: Cover! Petty officers, dismiss your divisions.

VOICE (*off*): Carpenters and gunners: Dismiss!

VOICE (*off*): Afterguardsmen: Dismiss!

VOICE (*off*): Fore, main, and mizzentopmen: Dismiss! (*The men break formation and go off, excepting* BUTLER, JENKINS, PAYNE, KINCAID *and* BILLY, *who gather near the ratlines, at the rail.*)

BUTLER: I suppose in this clear water you could see him go down for quite a way.

BILLY: We're moving slow in this calm.

JENKINS: There'll be wind enough before dawn.

BUTLER: And that's the end of Enoch Jackson. Over the side he goes, and his mates forget him.

JENKINS: Whatever's happened to Jackson, he ain't worried none. He's got a hundred fathoms over him to keep him warm and cosy.

BILLY: I'd rather be buried at sea than on the beach, when I come to die. Will you stand by the plank, Tom, so I'll shake a friendly hand before I sink? Oh! But it's dead I'll be then, come to think! (*All laugh.*)

PAYNE: Don't you worry none. By that time, you won't give a sailmaker's damn.

KINCAID: It's only living makes sense to me, anyhow.

BILLY: Aye, I like to live. Even when it seems bad, there's a lot that's good in it.

JENKINS: Maybe for you, Bill. You wouldn't know trouble if it come up and spit in your eye.

BILLY: Don't you try now, mate! You might miss, and I got a clean jumper on!

PAYNE: That's the way to be, if you ask me. There's always trouble, if you know where to look for it.

BUTLER: You don't have to see nothing if you close your eyes.

KINCAID: When I close my eyes I sleep sound as a drunk marine.

BILLY: Aye, after I roll in my hammock, it's one, two, three, and I'm deep down under.

JENKINS: Well, it's down under for me right now. Let's lay below.

KINCAID: Aye, we'll be on watch before long. Coming, Bill?

BILLY: I think I'll stay and watch the water for a while. I like to watch the sea at night.

JENKINS: Aye. It's deep and silent, and it can drown a man before he knows it.

BILLY: Sleep sound, mates. (*All but Jenkins go down the companion hatchway.*)

JENKINS: Billy: stay clear of Jimmy-Legs.

JENKINS *exits down the hatchway.* BILLY *is left alone staring over the side until* CLAGGART *enters. He does not see Billy, but stops near the quarterdeck ladder and gazes fixedly seaward.*

BILLY: Good evening, sir.

CLAGGART (*startled, then subtly sarcastic*): Good evening.

BILLY: Will it be all right if I stay topside a bit to watch the water?

CLAGGART: I suppose the Handsome Sailor may do many things forbidden to his messmates.

BILLY: Yes, sir. The sea's calm tonight, isn't it? Calm and peaceful.

CLAGGART: The sea's deceitful, boy: calm above, and underneath, a world of gliding monsters preying on their fellows. Murderers, all of them. Only the sharpest teeth survive.

BILLY: I'd like to know about such things, as you do, sir.

CLAGGART: You're an ingenuous sailor, Billy Budd. Is there, behind that youthful face, the wisdom pretty virtue has need of? Even the gods must know their rivals, boy; and Christ had first to recognize the ills before he cured 'em.

BILLY: What, sir?

CLAGGART: Never mind. But tell me this: how have you stomach to stand here and talk to me? Are you so innocent and ignorant of what I am? You know my reputation. Jenkins and the rest are witnesses, and certainly you've heard them talking to me. Half of them would knife me in the back some night and do it gladly; Jenkins is thinking of it. Doubtless he'll try one day. How do you dare, then? Have you not intelligence enough to be afraid of me? To hate me as all the others do?

BILLY: Why should I be afraid of you, sir? You speak to me friendly when we meet. I know some of the men . . . are fearful of you, sir, but I can't believe they're right about it.

CLAGGART: You're a fool, fellow. In time, you'll learn to fear me like the rest. Young you are, and scarcely used to the fit of your man's flesh.

BILLY: I know they're wrong, sir. You aren't like they say. Nobody could be so.

CLAGGART: So . . . ? So what, boy? Vicious, did you mean to say, or brutal? But they aren't wrong, and you would see it, but for those blue eyes that light so kindly on your fellow men.

BILLY: Oh, I've got no education, I know that. There must be a lot of things a man misses when he's ignorant. But learning's hard. Must be sort of lonely, too.

CLAGGART: What are you prating of, half-man, half-child? Your messmates crowd around, admire your yellow hair and your blue eyes, do tricks and favours for you out of love, and you talk about loneliness!

BILLY: I just noticed the way you were looking off to leeward as I came up, sir. Kind of sad, you were looking.

CLAGGART: Not sadness, boy. Another feeling, more like . . . pleasure. That's it. I can feel it now, looking at you. A certain . . . pleasure.

BILLY (*flattered*): Thank you, sir.

CLAGGART (*annoyed at Billy's incomprehension*): Pah.

BILLY: Just talking with you, sir, I can tell they're wrong about you. They're ignorant, like me.

CLAGGART: Compliment for compliment, eh, boy? Have you no heart for terror, fellow? You've seen this stick in use. Have you not got sense and spleen and liver to be scared, even to be cowardly?

BILLY: No, sir, I s'pose not. I like talking to you, sir. But please, sir, tell me something.

CLAGGART: I wonder if I can. Well, ask it.

BILLY: Why do you want us to believe you're cruel, and not really like everybody else?

CLAGGART: I think you are the only child alive who wouldn't understand if I explained; or else you'd not believe it.

BILLY: Oh, I'd believe you, sir. There's much I could learn from you: I never knew a man like you before.

CLAGGART (*slowly*): Do you – like me, Billy Budd?

BILLY: You've always been most pleasant with me, sir.

CLAGGART: Have I?

BILLY: Yes, sir. In the mess, the day I came aboard. And almost every day you have a pleasant word.

CLAGGART: And what I have said tonight, are these pleasant words?

BILLY: Yes, sir. I was wondering . . . could I talk to you between watches, when you've nothing else to do?

CLAGGART: You're a plausible boy, Billy. Aye, the nights are long, and talking serves to pass them.

BILLY: Thank you, sir. That would mean a lot to me.

CLAGGART: Perhaps to me as well. (*Drops his rattan.* BILLY *picks it up and hands it back to him.* CLAGGART *stares at it a moment, then at Billy.*) No. No! Charm me, too, would you! Get away!

BILLY (*surprised and puzzled*): Aye, sir. (*He exits down the hatchway. After a pause in which* CLAGGART *recovers his self-control* SQUEAK *appears.*)

CLAGGART (*without turning*): Come here. I thought I told you to put that new seaman Budd on report. Why was it not done?

SQUEAK: I tried, Mister Claggart, sir. I couldn't find nothing out of place. Gear all stowed perfect.

CLAGGART: Then disarrange it. You know the practice. I want him on report.

SQUEAK: Two of his messmates is ones nearly caught me at it before.

CLAGGART: Then be more careful. Now get along and see you make out something. (SQUEAK *scurries off belowdecks as* VERE *comes into sight on the quarterdeck.*)

VERE: Master-at-Arms. What is that man doing above decks?

CLAGGART: Ship's corporal, sir. A routine report.

VERE: There is nothing in this ship of so routine a nature that I do not concern myself in it. Remember that.

CLAGGART: Aye, aye, sir. With your permission, sir. (*Exit.* VERE *walks along the deck and scans the sails as* SEYMOUR *enters.*)

SEYMOUR: Fine evening, sir.

VERE: Yes, a fine evening, Seymour. How is the glass?

SEYMOUR: Falling, I believe, sir. I think we'll toss a little before morning. Well, I suppose I should be in my cabin inspecting the deck logs.

VERE: Stay for a moment, Seymour. In the days and nights to come, you and I will not often have an opportunity to stand easy and talk.

SEYMOUR: Aye, sir. I expect the French will put us to our stations any hour now.

VERE: Are you impressed by omens, Seymour? This seaman we've just buried: I think of him as an omen of some sort, a melancholy prologue to this voyage.

SEYMOUR: Aye, sir. Hard on the sailor, certainly, but that's the service. But we've been lucky in other ways. An accident, now, that's unavoidable.

VERE: It was more than an accident, Seymour.

SEYMOUR: This maintop sailor? How do you mean, sir?

VERE: The man was sent aloft sick, by the Master-at-Arms, contrary to my standing order. Budd, the new seaman, implied as much, and the maintop watch confirmed it. The Master-at-Arms lied to me.

SEYMOUR: What are you going to do, sir? What action can you take? He's a valuable man, one we can hardly do without as things are now.

VERE: I shall do nothing at present, only wait and observe him. No court-martial could do more than strip him of his rank for such misconduct. I will let him have his head until some act puts him squarely counter to the law, then let the law consume him.

SEYMOUR: Why trouble the natural order to no purpose? Shouldn't we let it be?

VERE: Must a man always shrug, let things alone and drift? Would to God I could take this power of mine and break him now, smash all the laws to powder and be a man again.

SEYMOUR: We must serve the law, sir, or give up the right and privilege of service. It's how we live.

VERE: Live? Oh, you're right. Below this deck are men who at a call skip on the hurling spars against the wind, at Beat-to-quarters run as if they willed it. Yet each of us steps alone within this pattern, this formal movement centred on itself. Men live and die, taken by pattern, born to it, knowing nothing. No man can defy the code we live by and not be broken by it.

SEYMOUR: You are the Captain, sir. You maintain that code.

VERE: Keep an order we cannot understand. That's true. The world demands it: demands that at the back of every peace-maker there be the gun, the gallows and the gaol. I talk of justice, and would turn the law gentle for those who serve here; but a Claggart stands in my shadow, for I need him. So the world goes, wanting not justice, but order . . . to be let alone to hug its own iniquities. Let a man work to windward of that law and he'll be hove down. No hope for him, none. (*Enter* WYATT.)

WYATT: Eight o'clock report, sir. Ship inspected and all in order.

SEYMOUR: Very well, carry on. (WYATT *goes off.*) By your leave, sir. Good night. (*Exit.* VERE *remains, crosses to the hatch and looks down, then slowly upward at the set of the sails.*)

SCENE 3

The maindeck several nights later.

Four bells is struck offstage. A sailor climbs wearily down the ratlines, drops to the deck and goes below. CLAGGART *stands by the larboard rail.*

As BILLY *enters from below decks, he sees the Master-at-Arms.*

BILLY: Hello, sir. (CLAGGART *looks at him without answering, then turns and goes off forward.* THE DANSKER *follows Billy up onto the deck.*) Well, that's all there is to tell, Dansker. I always lash my hammock just so, and stow my gear same as all the others. They don't get in trouble.

THE DANSKER: Mister Claggart is down upon you, Billy.

BILLY: Jimmy-Legs? Why, he calls me the sweet and pleasant fellow, they tell me.

THE DANSKER: Does he so, Baby lad? Aye, a sweet voice has Mister Claggart.

BILLY: For me he has. I seldom pass him but there comes a pleasant word.

THE DANSKER: And that's because he's down upon you.

BILLY: But he's my friend. I know he talks a little strange, but he's my friend.

THE DANSKER: Nobody's friend is Jimmy-Legs. Yours the least of all, maybe. Lay aloft, Baby. You'll be late to relieve your watch.

BILLY: Aye, Dansker. (*He climbs up the ratlines out of sight.* THE DANSKER *watches him go.* CLAGGART *appears, but* THE DANSKER *ignores him and goes off aft. As* JENKINS *comes into view climbing down the ratlines,* CLAGGART *gestures off and fades into a shadowy corner of the deck near the quarterdeck ladder.* SQUEAK *enters as* JENKINS *drops to the deck, and intercepts him as he starts down the companionway.)*

SQUEAK: It's all right, mate, slack off and stay a bit.

JENKINS: What do you want? I pick my own company.

SQUEAK: So does I, mate, so does I. And if I may make so bold to say it, you'll be smarter to pick your company more careful.

JENKINS: If you got something to say to me, talk up, else I'll get below.

SQUEAK: Don't be hasty, now, mate, don't be in a sweat. It's haste gets good men into trouble. What d'you think of our new hand here, Billy Boy? Mister Claggart's taken with him, too. Fine young fellow, ha?

JENKINS: Talk plain. What d'you mean?

SQUEAK: I overheard him talking just this day. Would maybe surprise you some, what he had to say about yourself and a few other lads.

JENKINS: What?

SQUEAK: Aoh, bit of talk about his messmates. He don't fancy us! Not like his feather boys aboard the merchantman.

JENKINS: You lying cut-throat, try something else! Billy's in my mess; since he come on board he's rare been out of my sight. You're lying, you bloody nark! I know you too well. You'll need to try some other way to get Bill into trouble. Get away, and don't come lying to me no more.

SQUEAK: Aoh, so it's that friendly you are! Well, now, ain't that sweet! You're not smart, Jenkins. Remember, man: I tried to help you out. When you're feeling the cat between your shoulders . . .

JENKINS (*seizing him*): Damn your lies! Get back to Jimmy-Legs and kiss his butt. And stay out of my way! (*Throws Squeak down and exits.* SQUEAK *watches him go.* CLAGGART *steps out of the shadows.)*

CLAGGART: I heard your little talk. You lack subtlety; but I'm the greater fool to use you in these matters. You're inept.

SQUEAK: Aoh! Why don't you do it yourself, if you don't need me!

CLAGGART: I need nobody, least of all a rum-soaked footpad from the Old Bailey. If you wish to have free rein with your distasteful habits, mind your cockney manners! I stand between you and the flogging whip. Improve your style, or you stand tomorrow forenoon at the gratings!

SQUEAK: I only meant as you could do it better, Mister Claggart, I wouldn't say nothing to . . .

CLAGGART (*cuts him on the arm with his rattan*): Don't touch me! – Keep Budd in petty troubles, that you can do. Unlash his hammock. Keep him on report. In time I'll let you know what plans I have for him. Get aft! (SQUEAK, *eager to get away, scuttles aft as* THE DANSKER *enters.*) Well, old man. Moon's in and out tonight. There's weather somewhere. (THE DANSKER *turns down the night lamp over the cabin door and starts off.*) Stay and have a pipe.

THE DANSKER: I have the watch.

CLAGGART: You take your duties as seriously as ever.

THE DANSKER: Aye. They are all of life for an old seaman like me. (*Turns to go.*)

CLAGGART: You move away from me as though I were some kind of stalking beast. You avoid me, too.

THE DANSKER: Your word, John, 'too'.

CLAGGART: You know what I mean. The hands detest me. You are a hand, older than most, and older in your hatred, I have no doubt. But why, man? You at least should see me as I am, a man who knows how the world's made: made as I am.

THE DANSKER: How can I know what goes on in your head?

CLAGGART: The enigmatic Dansker. Come, it's dark, we can drop disguises when night serves to hold the disclosing soul apart.

THE DANSKER: You know who you remind me of . . . main-topman: Billy Budd.

CLAGGART: More enigmas! That sunny, smiling infant with no spleen nor knowledge in his head?

THE DANSKER: I'll leave you now.

CLAGGART: No, stay a while. This is a night for secrets and disclosures.

THE DANSKER: You have half the truth and Billy Budd the other. He can't see there's evil in the world, and you won't see the good.

CLAGGART: So. And I take it you come in between.

THE DANSKER: I keep outside. I am too old to stand between sky and water.

CLAGGART: And yet you hate me, too.

THE DANSKER: I hate an incomplete man.

CLAGGART: Damn all this talk. Hate me and have done. Let it alone, I say. Whatever else it is, this thing is Man, still!

THE DANSKER: I'll be off.

CLAGGART: Don't go. The moon's gone under. Let us talk this out. You are a wise man in your senile way.

THE DANSKER: Then take this for all my wisdom. You recognize the hatred of your shipmates as an honour paid to a soul they cannot understand. Your fine contempt for human love is nothing but regret.

CLAGGART: Stop there. I know the rest by heart. Nothing you say to me but clatters in my belly, watch on watch. Aye: when this arm moves out in gesture of love, it mocks me with a blow. Who lifts this arm? What officer commands this hireling flesh? Somewhere below the farthest marks and deeps, God anchors hearts, and his sea rusts mine hollow. The flukes break in the bottom, and I slack and stand, go in and out forever at God's humour. Look at this sea: for all her easy swell, who knows what bones, ribs and decay are fathomed at her base and move in her motion, so that on the flattest water, the very stricture of the dead can kill that beauty with a dance of death? – Here is a man. He holds, past fathom curves, drowned fleets of human agonies that gesture when the long tide pulls.

THE DANSKER: Aye, John. But you must know that other men are moved so. Look up some evening at the quarterdeck for another poor thoughtful devil like you, like me, pacing all night between his doubts.

CLAGGART: What, Vere? That fine-drawn manner doesn't deceive me. There's a whited sepulchre, like all soft-spoken charmers of this world.

THE DANSKER: You don't believe in anything besides yourself, eh John?

CLAGGART: I've said what I have said. I know myself, and look to that. You should try it. Go to your post, old man, and your everlasting duties. (CLAGGART *turns away.* BILLY *scrambles into view down the ratlines and calls out excitedly.*)

BILLY: Quarterdeck ho!

RATCLIFFE (*coming forward to the forward break of the quarterdeck*): Sound off!

BILLY: Strange sail one mile off the larboard beam!

CLAGGART (*to The Dansker*): A Frenchman! Get to your station.

RATCLIFFE (*on the quarterdeck ladder*): Mister Duncan! Sound Beat-to-quarters! Clear for action!

DUNCAN (*offstage*): Aye aye, sir!

RATCLIFFE: Gardiner! (*Enter* GARDINER.)

GARDINER: Sir?

RATCLIFFE: Report to the Captain, strange sail on the larboard beam. Then send Payne to the wheel. (*Exit* GARDINER.) Master-at-Arms, send a man to the mast to relay lookout's reports. Inspect battle stations and report to me when they are fully manned.

CLAGGART: Aye aye, sir. (*Exit.*)

VOICE (*off*): She's a French frigate! Steering east by south! (*Enter* VERE *and* SEYMOUR.)

VERE: Prepare to make chase. Have your quartermaster steer small.

RATCLIFFE: Aye aye, sir.

Enter the DRUMMER *who sounds Beat-to-quarters. Men run on, to gun stations, rigging, crossing stage and off.*

SEYMOUR: She's too fast for us, sir. We'll never come up with her.

VERE: We are bound to try, though we were sure to fail. And we may smell powder before this chase is over.

CLAGGART (*re-entering*): Battle stations fully manned, sir!

SEYMOUR: May we try a shot at her now?

VERE: She's drawing south. Yes, commence firing, Mr Seymour.

SEYMOUR: Larboard battery, fire one!

DUNCAN: Fire! (*Fire one gun.*)

VERE: Fire at will!

SEYMOUR: Fire at will!

Guns fire dissynchronously.

ACT TWO

SCENE I

The quarterdeck and part of the maindeck a few minutes before 0800. A high wind. On the quarterdeck are LIEUTENANT WYATT, MIDSHIPMAN REA *and the helmsman,* STOLL.

REA: I'm glad this watch is over. I'm tired.

WYATT: Make your entry in the log before your relief comes up. Bring it out here and I'll sign it.

REA: Aye, sir. What was our last position, do you remember?

WYATT: Thirteen ten west, forty-three forty north.

REA: And an easterly breeze.

WYATT: Aye, make it so. That'll make Ratcliffe happy. Last time he had an east wind, she blew his hat over the side. And put down 'Running ground swell'.

REA: Aye aye, sir. (*Exits.*)

WYATT: Helmsman, keep her close-hauled.

STOLL: I can't, sir. Too much cloth in the wind.

WYATT: Well, hold her close as you can, and let the next watch reef sail if they like.

STOLL: Aye aye, sir. (*Enter* RATCLIFFE.)

WYATT: Morning, Johnny! You're on time!

RATCLIFFE: What's the course?

WYATT: Steady south. Wind's easterly. Glass is dropping.

RATCLIFFE: East wind? Damn it. (*Enter* BYREN, *the relief helmsman.*) By the way, you forgot to sign the order book.

WYATT: All right. Thanks.

STOLL: I've been relieved, sir. Byren has the helm.

WYATT: Very well. (*Exit* STOLL.) Who's mate of your watch?

RATCLIFFE: The Admiralty midshipman. That lobcock Gardiner, hang him. (*Eight bells.*)

WYATT: Where the devil is he? It's eight. (*Enter* REA *and* GARDINER *separately, meeting.*)

RATCLIFFE: There he comes. He looks happy. That means trouble for some poor devil. (GARDINER *snatches the log out of Rea's hands and bounds up to the quarterdeck.*)

REA: I've been relieved, sir. Horatio, Lord Gardiner has the watch.

WYATT: Ah, Midshipman Gardiner. The backbone of the British Navy.

RATCLIFFE: The backside, if you ask me.

WYATT: All right, Rea. You can turn in. (REA *exits.*)

RATCLIFFE: Pity we lost that Frenchman last night. A little action would season the monotony of these interminable watches.

WYATT: Did you ever hear of a ship-ot-the-line running down a frigate, even with the wind? Ah, it's a magnificent morning! Thickening overcast, heavy ground swell, a fresh levanter breeze, and you, Johnny, are the Pride of the Morning!

RATCLIFFE: Mmm. Has the skipper been on deck yet?

WYATT: Not since sunrise. He came up then and paced the deck and stared off east like a sleepwalker. Then went below again without a word.

RATCLIFFE: He thinks too much.

WYATT: Well, if you ever make captain, your crew won't have that to complain of, anyway. Am I relieved?

RATCLIFFE: Yes, I relieve you. (*Tosses his cap to Wyatt.*) Here. Take this below, will you?

WYATT: What? You'll be out of uniform, man. Mister Gardiner wouldn't approve of your standing watch without a hat, would you, Midshipman Gardiner?

GARDINER: Sir, the Articles state that officers on watch . . .

RATCLIFFE: Well, hang it, I lost twelve shillings the last time my hat went over the rail, and this is the only other one I've got. To hell with the Articles.

WYATT: Mind your language! It's downright mutinous. Well, don't expect me to stand your watches if you catch your death of cold. Good morning. (*Exit.*)

GARDINER: Midshipman Rea, sir, I don't like to say it, but his log entries are impossible.

RATCLIFFE: Then enter yourself, Mister Gardiner. So are you.

GARDINER: Yes sir. But I do think he ought to be told . . .

RATCLIFFE: Go find the Captain and report to him the wind's abeam. Respectfully suggest we ought to take in topsails.

GARDINER: Aye aye, sir. (*Goes down stairs.*)

RATCLIFFE: And don't forget to tell him I haven't got a hat.

GARDINER: What's that, sir?

RATCLIFFE: Nothing, sir! You got my order. Dump your ballast and shove off!

GARDINER: I thought you spoke to me, sir.

RATCLIFFE: I avoid that whenever possible. Move!

GARDINER: Yes, sir.

RATCLIFFE: Ye gods, what a brat. Nothing off, helmsman. She's well enough thus.

BYREN: Nothing off, sir.

GARDINER (*nearly bumping into* VERE *as he emerges from cabin, followed by* SEYMOUR *and* HALLAM): Atten-tion!

RATCLIFFE: Good morning, sir.

VERE: Morning, Mister Ratcliffe.

GARDINER (*starting after Vere, bumps into Hallam*): Damn it, man, watch what you're doing!

VERE: Midshipman Gardiner.

GARDINER: Sir?

VERE: How long, pray, have you been in this ship, or any ship?

GARDINER: This is my first cruise, sir.

VERE: Your first cruise. A wartime cruise as well. And you are a midshipman. A midshipman, Mister Gardiner, let me tell you, is neither fish, flesh, nor fowl, and certainly no seaman. You're a salt-water hermaphrodite, Mister Gardiner. And unless you have a mind to be generally known as Spit-kit Gardiner, I recommend more tolerance toward the men. Now, is that clear?

GARDINER: Aye aye, sir!

VERE: Very well, you may carry on.

RATCLIFFE: We've a weather helm, sir, and bow seas.

VERE: Take in topsails, if you please, Mister Ratcliffe.

RATCLIFFE: Aye aye, sir. Mister Duncan!

DUNCAN (*enters*): Aye, sir?

RATCLIFFE: Douse your topsails and topgallants. Haul in the weather braces.

DUNCAN: Aye aye, sir. (*Exit.*) Away aloft! Hands by topgallant sheets and halyards!

GARDINER: Aloft there! Keep fast the weather sheets till the yards are down, da . . . if you please!

RATCLIFFE: Get aloft yourself, Mister Gardiner, see they do it right, since you're not satisfied.

GARDINER: Sir, the Articles state that . . .

RATCLIFFE: Did you hear me?

GARDINER: Aye aye, sir. (*Exits up ratlines.*)

DUNCAN (*off*): Haul taut!

VERE: You disapprove of Gardiner, Mister Ratcliffe?

RATCLIFFE: He seems to think he's the only midshipman aboard capable of doing anything properly. He's always looking at you as if your hat weren't squared.

VERE: That is an unfortunate simile under the present circumstances.

RATCLIFFE (*caught*): Oh, I – er – Keep her close to the wind, helmsman. Don't fall away!

DUNCAN (*off*): Let go topgallant bowlines!

VERE: I think Gardiner has had enough correction for one day. Call him down to our level, Mister Ratcliffe.

RATCLIFFE: Aye, sir. Mister Gardiner! You may come off your perch now! (BILLY *descends rigging and starts offstage.*) What do you think of our new man Budd, Captain?

SEYMOUR: That boy did a smart piece of work for us last night, sir. He's the nimblest man on the tops I've ever watched. Wyatt wants him for captain of the foretop.

VERE: Very well, let Budd take the post. He certainly deserves it for his actions last night during the chase. I'll speak to him myself.

SEYMOUR: He'll like hearing it from you, sir.

VERE: Hallam, go call Budd, the lad moving forward there. (*Exit* HALLAM. GARDINER *appears, looking sick.*) Well done, Gardiner. You may lay below and draw an extra tot of rum. You look . . . chilly.

GARDINER: Thank you, sir. (*Exit.*)

SEYMOUR: By the way, sir, Budd has been on the Master-at-Arms' report once or twice for some petty misdemeanour. Nothing serious. (*Steps aside with Ratcliffe.* BILLY *enters, followed by* HALLAM.)

BILLY: You sent for me, sir?

VERE: Yes, Budd. Your division officer recommends you for a post of more responsibility. He thinks you can perform duties of a higher station, and so do I, after last night. So I've agreed that you shall have Williams' place on the foretop.

BILLY: But – Williams is captain of the foretop, sir.

VERE: The station calls for a younger man. Lieutenant Wyatt asked for you, and the spirit you showed last night warrants it. That is a real honour for a man so new on board.

BILLY: The Navy's new to me, Captain, but I hardly know anything else but the sea and ships.

VERE: And how do you like us, now that the awesomeness has worn away a bit?

BILLY: The Navy's a bustling world, sir. Bigger than the *Rights of Man*, and I get lost sometimes. But my mates lend me a hand. Why even Jimmy-Legs – beg pardon, sir, the Master-at-Arms, I mean – he's good to me, too.

VERE: The sea and the Navy exact a discipline, but it need not be a harsh one. In some ways I envy the man who dances across the tops and seems to rule the ship and sea below. Up there is a pleach of ropes for you to make a world of. Though winds have their way with tackle of your world, you live at ease against your strength and the round bole of the mast in your back. You are a king up there, while the water curds and frolics at the forefoot. I envy you that stance.

BILLY: You can trust me, Captain.

VERE: I do, boy. Very well, that's all.

BILLY: Aye aye, sir. Thank you, sir, thank you! (*Runs off.*)

VERE: Hallam, find the Master-at-Arms and bid him report to me.

HALLAM: Aye aye, sir. (*Exit.* SEYMOUR *joins Vere.*)

VERE: If I had a son, I'd hope for one like Budd.

SEYMOUR: Aye, sir. Fine boy. He's a force for order in this ship, certainly. I hope his charm's contagious.

VERE: One such is enough. Men cannot stand very much perfection. It's a disease that we stamp out at its first rash showing. (*Enter* CLAGGART. SEYMOUR *withdraws.*) Master-at-Arms, I want to make a change on the Watch, Quarter and Station Bill. I needn't have troubled you about it until later, but I am especially interested in this change.

CLAGGART: The time of day is indifferent to me, sir.

VERE: Williams, present captain of the foretop, is assigned to the afterguard. I am replacing him with Budd.

CLAGGART: William Budd, sir? You do not mean the so-called Handsome Sailor?

VERE: Aye, William Budd, the new seaman from the *Rights of Man*.

CLAGGART: I know him, sir.

VERE: Do you find anything unusual in this replacement?

CLAGGART: You must be aware, sir, that he is . . .

VERE: Well? That he is what? I know he's an able seaman.

CLAGGART: Nothing, sir. But I wondered if he were entirely trustworthy. He has been aboard such a brief time.

VERE: Long enough to prove himself to me, and to his shipmates.

CLAGGART: Very good, sir.

VERE: He is captain of the foretop. That is all.

CLAGGART: With your permission, sir. Will there not be some dissatisfaction among the foretopmen who have been aboard much longer than Budd?

VERE: Master-at-Arms: I concern myself with these matters. They are none of your function. Until such time as the senior topmen formally object to Budd for incapacity, he is captain of the foretop. Make it so on the Bill. (*Exits.*)

RATCLIFFE: What are you waiting for, man? Light to dawn? Promotion? You got the order.

CLAGGART: With your permission, sir.

As CLAGGART *goes off,* RATCLIFFE *spits over the rail.*

SCENE 2

Forward part of the deck. Night. Eight bells. A man descends the rigging and goes off. CLAGGART *enters, stands by the hatch for a moment, then exits forward.* BILLY *comes down off watch, drops to the deck and remains in shadow, leaning over the rail, looking seaward.* JENKINS *stealthily and silently comes up from below deck.*

BILLY: Jenkins! What you doing topside . . . (JENKINS *puts his hand over Billy's mouth.*)

JENKINS (*in a whisper*): Stow the noise! (*Releases Billy.*)

BILLY: You're after Mister Claggart, like you said you would!

JENKINS: Well? What about it? You try and stop me?

BILLY: He knows, Jenkins! I tell you, he knows! He's ready for you!

JENKINS: Then by God, I'll oblige him! I been waiting up here every night, waiting for him to come by when it's dark. Now get away and let me do it!

BILLY: No! I won't let you hang yourself!

JENKINS: I don't give a fiddler's damn what happens to me! Move out of my way, mate!

BILLY: No! Give me the knife.

JENKINS: The knife's for Claggart. You're a nice boy, Bill, but I ain't playing with you. You get away below, quick. This game ain't for boys.

BILLY: Damme, no, Jenkins! You'll hang yourself!

JENKINS: Take your hands off! The moon's under, I can do it now! Oh, sweet mother of God, leave me go!

BILLY: No!

JENKINS: Yes, by God!

JENKINS *strikes Billy; struggle, in which* BILLY *wrests knife from Jenkins, and it falls on deck.* BILLY *knocks Jenkins down.*

CLAGGART (*offstage*): What's that noise? Stand where you are! (*Entering.*) You again! Well? Explain this pageant.

BILLY: He . . . I had to hit him, sir. He struck at me.

CLAGGART: Mm. And drew that knife on you, too, no doubt.

BILLY: Yes, sir.

CLAGGART: I have been waiting, forward there, for Jenkins. You intercepted him, I take it.

BILLY: I didn't know you were looking for him, sir.

CLAGGART: You shouldn't meddle, my fine young friend, in matters that don't concern you! I was expecting him. (*Enter* THE DANSKER.) There, help the body up. I do not thank you, boy, for cheating me of the pleasure of his punishment.

WYATT (*offstage*): What's the disturbance there? You, forward on the spar-deck!

CLAGGART: Master-at-Arms reports all in order, sir!

WYATT (*offstage*): Stand where you are.

CLAGGART: The sweet and pleasant fellow saved you, Jenkins. But I reserve you still for my own justice in due time. Say nothing to this officer. (*Enter* WYATT.)

WYATT: What's the matter, Master-at-Arms? It's an odd hour for stargazing.

CLAGGART: A slight matter, sir. I found these two men together here on deck, contrary to the Captain's orders. I was sending them below when you called out.

WYATT: Oh, is that all. Carry on, then.

CLAGGART: Aye aye, sir. Now then, get below, both of you. (*Enter* VERE *followed by Hallam.* THE DANSKER *goes off.*) Attention!

VERE: Wyatt, what's this mean?

WYATT: Two men on deck without permission, sir.

VERE: Is there no more to this? The story's lame, man. What occurred? (*Silence.*) Very well, then. Go along, both of you.

BILLY: Aye aye, sir. Come along, mate. (*Exits with* JENKINS.)
VERE: Your knife, Master-at-Arms?
CLAGGART: William Budd's, sir, I believe.
VERE: Return it to him. (*Exits with Hallam and Wyatt.*)

CLAGGART *raps rail with rattan.* SQUEAK *approaches warily.*

CLAGGART: Listen carefully; you may make up for your late mistakes if you do this smartly. Give Budd just time enough to get to sleep. At four bells wake him. Bring him to the lee forechains. You understand?

SQUEAK: Mister Claggart, sir . . . we done enough to him. He's a good lad, Mister Claggart. Couldn't it be somebody else? Jenkins, maybe?

CLAGGART: So. He's softened your heart too, eh? Do as you're ordered, man, or I'll see your back laid raw with a flogging whip! Remember: I will be watching you. Bring him to the lee forechains. And when you're there . . .

SQUEAK: Dansker. Moving forward.

CLAGGART: Step back, you fool. Wait for me.

Exit SQUEAK. THE DANSKER *enters.*

THE DANSKER: Baby saved you, eh? And you are angry.

CLAGGART: Saved me, you say? From what? I've tried to tempt Jenkins to this blow, so as to break his toplofty spirit with his neck; and I am 'saved' by that guileless idiot! He'd turn the other cheek to me, in Christian kindness! Well: there's a second pleasure in striking that same face twice. I can destroy him, too, if I choose to do it!

THE DANSKER: Crazy, crazy!

CLAGGART: All right, old man, call it madness then. Whatever its name, it will plunder the sweetness from that face, or it will kill us both.

THE DANSKER: You are afraid of him.

CLAGGART: Afraid? Of Budd? What nonsense is that?

THE DANSKER: He usurps the crew; they turn from hating you to loving him, and leave you impotent.

CLAGGART: That bastard innocent frighten me! That witless kindness that spills from him has neither force nor aim. Stand out from between us, or you founder together, sink in five hundred fathoms with him, if I want it so!

THE DANSKER: Aye, then, if you take that tack, let it be both of us. You expect me to sit by and watch your deliberate arm seize him and force him under?

CLAGGART: Why not? You have always done that. I thought your practice was to stay outside. What breeds the saintly knight errant in you?

THE DANSKER: I am old, but I have some manhood left.

CLAGGART: What can you do? You've drifted with the tide too long, old one. You are as involved as I am now.

THE DANSKER: So you may say. In this ship a man lives as he can, and finds a way to make life tolerable for himself. I did so. That was a fault. But no longer.

CLAGGART: Stand clear. You haven't courage to cross me.

THE DANSKER: Eh, I'm not afraid of you; I see your scheme.

CLAGGART: Damn your feeble, ineffectual eyes! (*Striking him;* THE DANSKER *falls.*) You can see only what I let you see!

THE DANSKER: Say what you like. I see your scheme; so will Captain if need be.

CLAGGART (*pulling him to his feet*): Take a warning for yourself, old man. And keep away! You are on watch, eh? Well, go back to sleep again, or I'll report you. (THE DANSKER *exits.* CLAGGART *watches him go, then violently breaks his rattan and throws the pieces over the side.*)

SCENE 3

Forward part of the main deck. Four bells. CLAGGART *stands with one hand on the rail, waiting. After a short pause, hearing a sound, he fades into shadow.* SQUEAK *enters, bending over and running.*

SQUEAK: Hsssssssssst! (BILLY, *sleepy and rubbing his eyes, enters.*)

BILLY: You brought me all the way up here, out of my hammock. Now what do you want?

SQUEAK: I heard you're captain of the foretop, Bill. That right?

BILLY: Aye. What's that to do with you?

SQUEAK: Ah, now you can be more use to your shipmates than ever you was before.

BILLY: What?

SQUEAK: You was impressed, now, weren't you? Well, so was I. We're not the only impressed ones, Billy. There's a gang of us. Could you help . . . at a pinch?

BILLY: What do you mean?

SQUEAK: See here . . . (*Holds up two coins.*) Here's two gold guineas for you, Bill. Put in with us. Most of the men aboard are only waiting for a word, and they'll follow you. There's more for you where these come from. What d'you say? If you join us, Bill, there's not a man aboard won't come along! Are you with us? The ship'll be ours when we're ready to take it!

BILLY: Damme, I don't know what you're driving at, but you had better go where you belong! (SQUEAK, *surprised, does not move.* BILLY *springs up.*) If you don't start, I'll toss you back over the rail! (SQUEAK *decamps.* BILLY *watches him and starts off himself.* THE DANSKER, *offstage, calls out.*)

THE DANSKER: Hallo, what's the matter? (*Enters.*) Ah, Beauty, is it you again? Something must have been the matter, for you stammered. (CLAGGART *appears and comes forward.*)

CLAGGART: You seem to favour the maindeck, Billy Budd. What brings you topside at this hour, man, against my orders and the Captain's?

BILLY: I . . . found an afterguardsman in our part of the ship here, and I bid him be off where he belongs.

THE DANSKER: And is that all you did about it, boy?

BILLY: Aye, Dansker, nothing more.

CLAGGART: A strange sort of hour to police the deck. Name the afterguardsman.

BILLY: I . . . can't say, Mister Claggart. I couldn't see him clear enough.

THE DANSKER: Don't be a fool, speak up, accuse him.

CLAGGART: Well?

BILLY: I can't say, sir.

CLAGGART: You refuse? Then get below, and stay where you belong.

BILLY: Aye aye, sir. Good night, sir. Good night, Dansker. (*Exits.*)

CLAGGART: I'm glad you saw this mutinous behaviour.

THE DANSKER: Your crazy brain squeezes out false conclusions. He has done nothing except find you out, though he's too innocent to know it.

CLAGGART: I am not hoodwinked by his weak excuse. What else would he be doing at this hour, but fanning rebel tempers like his own?

THE DANSKER: I stood in the shadows forward when your pander Squeak slipped by me, running from this place. You set him on, on purpose to trap Billy.

CLAGGART: And I will do that, old man. But you will say nothing about it; see you don't. (*Enter* VERE *followed by* HALLAM.)

VERE: Well, Master-at-Arms. You stand long watches.

CLAGGART: Sir. May I take the liberty of reserving my explanation for your private ear. I believe your interest in this matter would incline you to prefer some privacy.

VERE (*to The Dansker and Hallam*): Leave us. Hallam, stand within hail. (THE DANSKER *and* HALLAM *go off.*) Well? What is it you wish to say, Master-at-Arms?

CLAGGART: During my rounds this night, I have seen enough to convince me that one man aboard, at least, is dangerous; especially in a ship which musters some who took a guilty part in the late serious uprisings . . .

VERE: You may spare a reference to that.

CLAGGART: Your pardon, sir. Quite lately I have begun to notice signs of some sort of movement secretly afoot, and prompted by the man in question. I thought myself not warranted, so long as this suspicion was only indistinct, in reporting it. But recently . . .

VERE: Come to the point, man.

CLAGGART: Sir, I deeply feel the cruel responsibility of making a report involving such serious consequences to the sailor mainly concerned. But God forbid, sir, that this ship should suffer the experience of the Nore.

VERE: Never mind that! You say there is one dangerous man. Name him.

CLAGGART: William Budd, the . . . captain of the foretop.

VERE: William Budd?

CLAGGART: The same, sir. But for all his youth and appealing manners, a secret, vicious lad.

VERE: How, vicious?

CLAGGART: He insinuates himself into the good will of his mates so that they will at least say a word for him, perhaps even take action with him, should it come to that. With your pardon, sir; you note but his fair face; under that there lies a man-trap.

VERE (*after a pause*): Master-at-Arms, I intend to test your accusation here and now. Hallam! (*Enter* HALLAM.)

HALLAM: Aye, sir.

VERE: Find Budd, the foretopman. Manage to tell him out of earshot that he is wanted here. Keep him in talk yourself. Go along.

HALLAM: Aye aye, sir. (*Exits.*)

VERE (*angry and perturbed*): Do you come to me with such a foggy tale, Master-at-Arms? As to William Budd, cite me an act, or spoken word of his, confirming what you here in general charge against him. Wait; weigh what you speak. Just now, and in this case, there is the yardarm end for false witness.

CLAGGART: I understand, sir. Tonight, when on my rounds, discovering Budd's hammock was unused, I combed the ship, and found him in conclave with several growlers; men, who, like himself, spread unrest and rebellion in the crew. They were collected here, near the lee forechains, and when I ordered them below, young Budd and others threatened me, and swore they'd drop me, and some officers they hate, overboard, some misty night. Should you, sir, desire substantial proof, it is not far.

Enter HALLAM, *followed by* BILLY.

VERE: Hallam, stand apart and see that we are not disturbed. (HALLAM *exits.*) And now, Master-at-Arms, tell this man to his face what you told me of him.

CLAGGART (*moving near to Billy, and looking directly at him*): Certainly, sir. I said this man, this William Budd, acting so out of angry resentment against impressment and his officers, against this ship, this Service, and the King, breeds in the crew a spirit of rebellion against the officers, the mates, and me, urging some outrage like the late revolt. I myself have seen and heard him speak with manifest malingerers and men who growl of mistreatment, harshness, unfair pay and similar complaints. I say this man threatened his officers with murder, and was bent tonight on urging other men to act concertedly in mutiny. I have nothing further to say, sir.

BILLY (*tries to speak, but can make only incoherent sounds. He seems to be in pain from the contortions of his face and the gurgling which is all he can effect for speech.*)

VERE: Speak, man, speak! Defend yourself! (*Remembering Billy's impediment, goes to him and puts a hand on his shoulder reassuringly.*) There is no hurry, boy. Take your time, take your time.

After agonized dumb gesturing and stammering, increased by Vere's kindness, BILLY'S *arm hits out at Claggart.* CLAGGART *staggers, falls, lies still.*

VERE: Stand back, man! It was a lie, then! (BILLY, *shaking, only stares at the body.* VERE *raises the body to a sitting position. Since Claggart remains inert,* VERE *lowers him again slowly, then rises.* BILLY *tries again to speak, without success; he is crying and badly frightened.*) No need to speak now, Billy. Hallam! (*Enter* HALLAM.) Tell the Surgeon I wish to see him here at once. And bid Mister Seymour report to my cabin without delay. (*To Billy.*) Retire to the stateroom aft. Remain there till I summon you. (BILLY *exits.* VERE *waits, turning once to stare at Claggart's body. Enter the* SURGEON.) Surgeon, tell me how it is with him. (SURGEON *bends over Claggart briefly, then looks up in surprise.*) Come, we must dispatch. Go now. I shall presently call a drumhead court to try the man who out of God's own instinct dropped him there. Tell the lieutenants that a foretopman has, in an accidental fury, killed this man. Inform the Captain of Marines as well, and charge them to keep the matter to themselves. (SURGEON *exits.*) The divine judgment of Ananias! Struck dead by the Angel of God . . . and I must judge the Angel. Can I save him? Have I that choice?

ACT THREE

SCENE I

Captain Vere's cabin, a quarter of an hour later. VERE *and* SEYMOUR.

SEYMOUR: Budd beat a man to death! What had he done?

VERE: Lied again: lied to Budd's face, hoping to kill him by it. Oh, the boy was tempted to it past endurance.

SEYMOUR: False witness has its penalty, sir. Budd has set our justice right.

VERE: Aye, too right. This natural, right act, done in an instinct's fever of recognition, was late and fatal.

SEYMOUR: What are you going to do, Captain? Isn't this last lie of the Master-at-Arms the very act you were waiting for, so as to let the law destroy him, as you said? He should have suffered at the yardarm if Billy hadn't killed him.

VERE: Yes. He should. But by fair process of authority. Budd has prevented that, and turned the law against himself.

SEYMOUR: You can't condemn the boy for answering with his arm for lack of words! The motive was clearly justified.

VERE: Aye, but was the act? For God's sake try, try to convince me I am wrong!

SEYMOUR: This Master-at-Arms, you knew him for a liar, a vicious dog.

VERE: A dog's obeyed in office. Claggart was authority.

SEYMOUR: Then authority's an evil!

VERE: It often is. But it commands, and no man is its equal, not Billy, nor I. It will strike us down, and rightly, if we resist it.

SEYMOUR: Rightly! What power gives evil its authority? We

should thank God the man's dead, and the world well rid of that particular devil.

VERE: Our life has ways to hedge its evil in. No one must go above them; even innocents. Laws of one kind or other shape our course from birth to death. These are the laws pronouncing Billy's guilt; Admiralty codes are merely shadows of them.

SEYMOUR: That's tyranny, not law, forcing conformity to wrongs, giving the victory to the devil himself!

VERE: I thought so once. But without this lawful tyranny, what should we have but worse tyranny of anarchy and chaos? So aboard this man-of-war. Oh, if I were a man alone, manhood would declare for Billy.

SEYMOUR: Then do it. Put your strength and your authority behind Budd, and let him go.

VERE: When I think I could have watched him grow in comely wholeness of manhood . . . all lost now. What could have been, quenched in evil, swept out by that undertow.

SEYMOUR: It's more than anyone can have to answer for, Captain; to his peers, or to his God. Let him go free and try on mortal flesh! Will you urge a noose for him, marked like a common felon, and that devil still to have his wish, killing the boy at last?

VERE: Can I do otherwise? I'd give my life to save his, if I could.

SEYMOUR: It's in your hands, Captain. Only you can help him now.

VERE: Billy, Billy. What have we done to you? (*Knock.*) Yes, come in. (*Enter* HALLAM.)

HALLAM: Lieutenants Ratcliffe and Wyatt, sir.

VERE: Let them come in. (*Enter* RATCLIFFE *and* WYATT.)

SEYMOUR: You both know why you've been summoned hither?

WYATT: Yes, sir.

RATCLIFFE: Aye, sir, in a general sort of way.

SEYMOUR: Then take your chairs. Ratcliffe. You here, Wyatt. You are appointed members of a court-martial convened under extraordinary circumstances by Captain Vere. I am Senior Member, and I declare this court open. (WYATT, RATCLIFFE, *and* SEYMOUR *sit.* VERE *remains standing, apart.*) Sentry, bring the prisoner in. (HALLAM *salutes and exits.*) As you know, the Master-at-Arms has been killed by the foretopman, Budd. Whether by accident or by design, and whether the act shall carry the penalty of death or no, you are to decide. There is only one witness, Captain Vere. I shall call upon him to give his deposition as soon as the sentry brings in the prisoner. (*An uneasy silence.*)

WYATT: Budd wouldn't kill a minnow without good reason.

RATCLIFFE: What did the . . .

SEYMOUR: I had rather you did not express an opinion until after you have heard the evidence. (*Another awkward silence.* HALLAM *finally enters with* BILLY.) Sentry, stand outside. (*Exit* HALLAM.) You may sit down.

BILLY: Th-th-thank you, sir.

SEYMOUR: Captain: will you be good enough to give us your account?

VERE (*turning towards them*): I speak not as your Captain, but as witness before this court. The Master-at-Arms early this morning detailed to me an account of mutinous sentiments expressed by Budd, and in particular, spoke of overhearing a specific conversation last night on the mid-watch. He alleged that Budd offered him violence and threatened further violence against the officers.

WYATT: Budd a mutineer! That's absurd, he's the best-liked man . . .

SEYMOUR: Lieutenant Wyatt. Please do not interrupt the witness.

RATCLIFFE: Did the Master-at-Arms specify who the other malcontents were, sir?

VERE: He did not. He said merely that he was in possession of substantial proof of his accusation.

SEYMOUR: With your permission, sir . . . Budd, did you speak with anyone in the Master-at-Arms' hearing last night?

BILLY: I . . . spoke a little . . . with the Dansker, sir.

WYATT: Who is the Dansker?

BILLY: He's just called the Dansker, sir. He's always called so.

RATCLIFFE: I know him. A mainmast sailor.

SEYMOUR: Sentry. (*Enter* HALLAM.)

HALLAM: Sir.

SEYMOUR: Do you know a mainmast sailor referred to as 'the Dansker'?

HALLAM: Aye, sir.

SEYMOUR: Go on deck and find him. Let him know apart that he is wanted here, and arrange it so that none of the other people notice his withdrawing. See you do it tactfully. I want no curiosity aroused among the men.

HALLAM: Aye aye, sir. (*Exits.*)

SEYMOUR: Please go on.

VERE: I sent at once for Budd. I ordered the Master-at-Arms to be present at this interview, to make his accusation to Budd's face.

RATCLIFFE: May I ask what was the prisoner's reaction on being confronted by the Master-at-Arms?

VERE: I perceived no sign of uneasiness in his demeanour. I believe he smiled.

RATCLIFFE: And for the Master-at-Arms?

VERE: When I directed him to repeat his accusation, he faced Budd and did so.

WYATT: Did Budd reply?

VERE: He tried to speak, but could not frame his words.

SEYMOUR: And then, sir?

VERE: He answered with blows, and his accuser fell. . . . It was apparent at once that the attack was fatal, but I summoned the Surgeon to verify the fact. That is all. (*Turns away.*)

SEYMOUR (*to Billy*): You have heard Captain Vere's account. Is it, or is it not, as he says?

BILLY: Captain Vere tells the truth. It is just as Captain Vere says, but it is not as the Master-at-Arms said. I have eaten the King's bread, and I am true to the King.

VERE: I believe you, boy.

BILLY: God knows . . . I . . . thank you, sir.

SEYMOUR: Was there any malice between you and the Master-at-Arms?

BILLY: I bore no malice against the Master-at-Arms. I'm sorry he is dead. I did not mean to kill him. If I'd found my tongue, I would not have struck him. But he lied foully to my face, and I . . . had to say . . . something . . . and I could only say it . . . with a blow. God help me.

SEYMOUR: One question more – you tell us that what the Master-at-Arms said against you was a lie. Now, why should he have lied with such obvious malice, when you have declared that there was no malice between you? (BILLY *looks appealingly at Vere.*) Did you hear my question?

BILLY: I . . . I . . .

VERE: The question you put to him comes naturally enough. But can he rightly answer it? Or anyone else, unless, indeed, it be he who lies within there. (*Knock and enter immediately* HALLAM.)

HALLAM: The mainmast man, sir.

SEYMOUR: Send him in. (HALLAM *nods off and* THE DANSKER *enters.* HALLAM *withdraws, closing door.*) State your name and station.

THE DANSKER: I have no name. I'm called the Dansker, that's all I know. Mainmast man.

SEYMOUR: You have been summoned in secrecy to appear as

a witness before this court, of which I am Senior Member. I may not at this time disclose to you the nature of the offence being tried. However, the offender is William Budd, foretopman. (*Pause.*) Do you consent to give this court your testimony, though ignorant of the case at trial, and further, to keep in strictest confidence all that passes here?

THE DANSKER: Aye.

SEYMOUR (*pushes forward a Bible*): Do you so swear?

THE DANSKER (*touching the Bible*): I do.

SEYMOUR: Then this is my question. In your opinion, is there malice between Budd and the Master-at-Arms?

THE DANSKER: Aye.

VERE (*wheeling around*): How!

SEYMOUR: Explain your statement.

THE DANSKER: How should he not have hated him?

SEYMOUR: Be plain, man. We do not deal in riddles here.

THE DANSKER: Master-at-Arms bore malice towards a grace he could not have. There was no reason for it.

RATCLIFFE: In other words, this malice was one-sided?

THE DANSKER: Aye.

RATCLIFFE: And you cannot explain how it arose?

THE DANSKER: Master-at-Arms hated Billy . . .

SEYMOUR: One moment. I notice that you have been using the past tense in your testimony. Why?

THE DANSKER: I look around and sense finality here.

WYATT: You cannot explain further the cause of Claggart's hate for Budd?

THE DANSKER: Master-at-Arms made his world in his own image. Pride was his demon, and he kept it strong by others' fear of him. Billy could not imagine such a nature, saw nothing but a lonely man, strange, but a man still, nothing to be feared. So Claggart, lest his world be proven false, planned Billy's death. The final reason is beyond my thinking.

VERE: Aye, that is thoughtfully put. There is a mystery in iniquity. But it seems to me, Seymour, that the point we seek here is hardly material.

SEYMOUR: Aye, sir. Very well, you may go.

THE DANSKER: One thing more. Since this Master-at-Arms first came on board from God knows where, I have seen his shadow lengthen along the deck, and being under it, I was afraid. Whatever happened here, I am in part to blame – more than this lad. (*To Billy.*) I am an old man, Billy. You – try to – forgive me. (*Exits.*)

SEYMOUR: Have you any further questions to put to the accused?

RATCLIFFE: No.

WYATT: None.

SEYMOUR: William Budd, if you have anything further to say for yourself, say it now.

BILLY (*after glance at* VERE): I have said all, sir.

SEYMOUR: Sentry. (*Enter* HALLAM.) Remove the prisoner to the after compartment. (HALLAM *and* BILLY *exit. A long pause.*) Have you anything to say, Ratcliffe?

RATCLIFFE: Yes, sir. Claggart was killed because Budd couldn't speak. In that sense, that he stammers, he's a cripple. You don't hang a man for that, for speaking the only way he could.

WYATT: If you condemn him, it's the same thing as condoning the apparent lie the Master-at-Arms clearly told. I'd have struck him, too. The boy is clearly innocent, struck him in self-defence.

RATCLIFFE: Aye. I'm ready to acquit him now.

SEYMOUR: Good. Then we can reach a verdict at once.

VERE: Hitherto I have been a witness at this trial, no more. And I hesitate to interfere, except that at this clear crisis you ignore one fact we cannot close our eyes to.

SEYMOUR: With your pardon, sir, as Senior Member of this

court, I must ask if you speak now as our commanding officer or as a private man.

VERE: As convening authority, Seymour. I summoned this court, and I must review its findings and approve them before passing them on to the Admiralty.

SEYMOUR: Aye, sir, that is your right.

VERE: No right. Which of us here has rights? It is my duty, and I must perform it. Budd has killed a man – his superior officer.

SEYMOUR: We have found a verdict, sir.

VERE: I know that, Seymour. Your verdict sets him free, and so would I wish to do. But are we free to choose as we would do if we were private citizens? The Admiralty has its code. Do you suppose it cares who Budd is? Who you and I are?

SEYMOUR: We don't forget that, sir. But surely Claggart's tales were simply lies. We've established that.

VERE: Aye. But the Nore and Spithead were brute facts, and must not come again. The men were starved out before, but if they should think we are afraid . . .

RATCLIFFE: Captain, how could they? They certainly know Budd is no mutineer.

WYATT: Of course not. Since he came on board, he's done more to keep the crew in hand than any of us.

SEYMOUR: That's true. The men took naturally to him.

VERE: As officers we are concerned to keep this ship effective as a weapon. And the law says what we must do in such a case as this. Come now, you know the facts, and the Mutiny Act's provisions. At sea, in time of war, an impressed man strikes his superior officer, and the blow is fatal. The mere blow alone would hang him, at least according to the Act. Well then, the men on board know that as well as you and I. And we acquit him. They have sense, they know the proper penalty to follow, and yet it does not follow.

SEYMOUR: But they know Budd, sir, and Claggart too, I daresay. Would they not applaud the decision that frees Budd? They would thank us.

WYATT: String him to a yard, and they'll turn round and rescue him, and string us up instead!

RATCLIFFE: Aye, that's a point. It's twice as dangerous to hang the boy as it would be to let him go. If there's a mutinous temper in the crew, condemning Budd would surely set it off.

VERE: That is possible. Whatever step we take, the risk is great; but it is ours. That is what makes us officers. Yet if in fear of what our office demands we shirk our duty, we only play at war, at being men. If by our lawful rigour mutiny comes, there is no blame for us. But if in fear, miscalled a kind of mercy, we pardon Budd against specific order, and then the crew revolts, how culpable and weak our verdict would appear! The men on board know what our case is, how we are haunted by the Spithead risings. Have they forgotten how the panic spread through England? No. Your clemency would be accounted fear, and they would say we flinch from practising a lawful rigour lest new outbreaks be provoked. What shame to us! And what a deadly blow to discipline!

RATCLIFFE: I concede that, sir. But this case is exceptional, and pity, if we are men, is bound to move us, Captain.

VERE: So am I moved. Yet we cannot have warm hearts betraying heads that should be cool. In such a case ashore, an upright judge does not allow the pleading tears of women to touch his nature. Here at sea, the heart, the female in a man, weeps like a woman. She must be ruled out, hard though it be. (*Pause.*) Still silent? Very well, I see that something in all your downcast faces seems to urge that not alone the heart moves hesitancy. Conscience, perhaps. The private conscience moves you.

WYATT: Aye, that's it, sir. How can we condemn this man and

live at peace again within ourselves? We have our standards; ethics, if you like.

VERE: Challenge your scruples! They move as in a dusk. Come, do they import something like this: if we are bound to judge, regardless of palliating circumstances, the death of Claggart as the prisoner's deed, then does that deed appear a capital crime whereof the penalty is mortal? But can we adjudge to summary and shameful death a fellow creature innocent before God, and whom we feel to be so? Does that state the case rightly?

SEYMOUR: That is my feeling, sir.

VERE: You all feel, I am sure, that the boy in effect is innocent; that what he did was from an unhappy stricture of speech that made him speak with blows. And I believe that, too; believe as you do, that he struck his man down, tempted beyond endurance. Acquit him, then, you say, as innocent?

RATCLIFFE: Exactly! Oh I know the Articles prescribe death for what Budd has done, but that . . .

WYATT: Oh, stow the Articles! They don't account for such a case as this. You yourself say Budd is innocent.

VERE: In intent, Wyatt, in intent.

WYATT: Does that count for nothing? His whole attitude, his motive, count for nothing? If his intent . . .

VERE: The intent or non-intent of Budd is nothing to the purpose. In a court more merciful than martial it would extenuate, and shall, at the last Assizes, set him free. But here we have these alternatives only: condemn or let go.

SEYMOUR: But it seems to me we've got to consider the problem as a moral one, sir, despite the fact that we're not moralists. When Claggart told you his lie, the case immediately went beyond the scope of military justice.

VERE: I, too, feel that. But do these gold stripes across our arms attest that our allegiance is to Nature?

RATCLIFFE: To our country, sir.

VERE: Aye, Ratcliffe; to the King. And though the sea, which is inviolate Nature primeval, though it be the element whereon we move and have our being as sailors, is our official duty hence to Nature? No. So little is that true that we resign our freedom when we put this on. And when war is declared, are we, the fighters commissioned to destroy, consulted first?

WYATT: Does that deny us the right to act like men? We're not trying a murderer, a dockside cut-throat!

VERE: The gold we wear shows that we serve the King, the Law. What does it matter that our acts are fatal to our manhood, if we serve as we are forced to serve? What bitter salt leagues move between our code and God's own judgments! We are conscripts, every one, upright in this uniform of flesh. There is no truce to war born in the womb. We fight at command.

WYATT: All I know is that I can't sit by and see Budd hanged!

VERE: I say we fight by order, by command of our superiors. And if our judgments approve the war, it is only coincidence. And so it is with all our acts. So now, would it be so much we ourselves who speak as judges here, as it would be martial law operating through us? For that law, and for its rigour, we are not responsible. Our duty lies in this: that we are servants only.

RATCLIFFE: The Admiralty doesn't want service like that. What good would it do? Who'd profit by Budd's death?

WYATT: You want to make us murderers!

SEYMOUR: Wyatt! Control yourself!

VERE: What is this vessel that you serve in, Wyatt, an ark of peace? Go count her guns; then tell your conscience to lie quiet, if you can.

RATCLIFFE: But that is war. This would be downright killing!

SEYMOUR: It's all war, Ratcliffe; war to the death, for all of us.

VERE: You see that, Seymour? That this war began before our time?

SEYMOUR: And will end long after it.

VERE: Here we have the Mutiny Act for justice. No child can own a closer tie to parent than can that Act to what it stems from: War. This is a wartime cruise and in this ship are Englishmen who fight against their wills, perhaps against their conscience, 'pressed by war into the service of the King. Though we as fellow creatures understand their lot, what does it matter to the officer, or to the enemy? The French will cut down conscripts in the same swath with volunteers, and we will do as much for them. War has no business with anything but surfaces. War's child, the Mutiny Act, is featured like the father.

RATCLIFFE: Couldn't we mitigate the penalty if we convict him?

VERE: No, Ratcliffe. The penalty is prescribed.

RATCLIFFE: I'd like to think it over, Captain. I'm not sure.

VERE: I repeat, then, that while we ponder and you hesitate over anxieties I confess to sharing, the enemy comes nearer. We must act, and quickly. The French close in on us; the crew will find out shortly what has happened. Our consciences are private matters, Ratcliffe. But we are public men, controlling life and death within this world at sea. Tell me whether or not in our positions we dare let our consciences take precedence of the code that makes us officers and calls this case to trial.

RATCLIFFE (*after a pause; quietly*): No, sir.

WYATT: Can you stand Budd's murder on your conscience?

SEYMOUR: Wyatt! Hold your tongue!

WYATT (*jumping up*): I say let him go!

SEYMOUR: Sit down, sir!

VERE: Let him speak.

WYATT: I won't bear a hand to hang a man I know is innocent!

My blood's not cold enough. I can't give the kind of judgment you want to force on us! I ask to be excused from sitting upon this court.

SEYMOUR: Do you know what you're saying? Sit down and hold your tongue, man!

VERE: The kind of judgment I ask of you is only this, Wyatt: that you recognize your function in this ship. I believe you know it quite as well as we, yet you rebel. Can't you see that you must first strip off the uniform you wear, and after that your flesh, before you can escape the case at issue here? Decide you must, Wyatt. Oh, you may be excused and wash your hands of it, but someone must decide. We are the law; law orders us to act, and shows us how. Do you imagine Seymour, or Ratcliffe here, or I, would not save this boy if we could see a way consistent with our duties? Acquit Budd if you can. God knows I wish I could. If in your mind as well as in your heart, you can say freely that his life is not forfeit to the law we serve, reason with us! Show us how to save him without putting aside our function. Or if you can't do that, teach us to put by our responsibility and not betray ourselves. Can you do this? Speak, man, speak! Show us how! Save him, Wyatt, and you save us all. (WYATT *slowly sits down.*) You recognize the logic of the choice I force upon you. But do not think me pitiless in thus demanding sentence on a luckless boy. I feel as you do for him. But even more, I think there is a grace of soul within him that shall forgive the law we bind him with, and pity us, stretched on the cross of choice. (*Turns away.*)

SEYMOUR: Well, gentlemen. Will you decide? (*Officers write their verdicts on paper before them, and hand them to* SEYMOUR, *who rises, draws his dirk and places it on the table, pointing forward.*) He is condemned, sir. Shall we appoint the dawn?

SCENE 2

Captain Vere's cabin, 0400. Ship's bell strikes offstage. VERE *sitting alone at his desk. Knock at the door.*

VERE: Come in. (*Enter* SEYMOUR.) Oh, it's you, Seymour.

SEYMOUR: It's eight bells, Captain.

VERE: What's the hour of sunrise?

SEYMOUR: Four fifty-two, sir.

VERE: Eight bells. And one bell at four-thirty. Odd and even numbers caught between two hands. Budd shall not live to hear the odd made even or wrong made right. – Call all hands to quarters at four-thirty.

SEYMOUR: Aye aye, Captain. (*Turns irresolutely.*)

VERE: The wind has slackened, I think. How is the glass?

SEYMOUR: It's risen slightly. Sea has flattened out.

VERE: Fair weather after foul . . . it's all nature, nature and law. How exigent are these Mediterranean climates of the heart, and temperate zones of mind!

SEYMOUR: Have you been here all night, sir?

VERE: All night, Seymour . . . all my life moving between dark and dark. It has been a long night, but day will be quick and deadly on the mainyard. D'you think, Seymour, a man can forgive a wrong done of the heart's own election?

SEYMOUR: Most people are decent enough. You can forgive them trespasses.

VERE: No, by God. There's wickedness alive. It's dead now in one man, but it's alive to feel and smell at night. . . . Seymour, go below. Get Budd and bring him here.

SEYMOUR: But Captain . . .

VERE: Do as you're told. Get Budd and bring him here.

(SEYMOUR *exits.* VERE *sits motionless for a few moments, then rises and goes to the cabin door.*) Sentry.

HALLAM: Yes, sir?

VERE: Who has the deck this watch?

HALLAM: Mister Ratcliffe, Captain.

VERE: Very well. (*Pause.*) Sentry!

HALLAM: Sir?

VERE: When Mister Seymour has returned, admit him right away.

HALLAM: Aye aye, Captain.

VERE: The wind's still sharp. You must be cold there, Hallam. Go to the leeward side. I'll be responsible.

HALLAM: Thank you, sir. This is the coldest hour now, just before sunrise.

VERE (*closes door, returns slowly to his desk*): The lamp holds steady when the vessel heels. Does the law hang straight in crooked lives? It burns, and shapes nothing but shadows here, plumb in the twisting cabin of the mind. (*Footsteps, voices,* VERE *turns to door. Enter* SEYMOUR, BILLY, *and* HALLAM.) Take off the manacles. (HALLAM *frees Billy.*)

SEYMOUR (*to Hallam*): Outside, man. Bear a hand. (*Exits with Hallam.*)

VERE: Sit down. No, it's better that I stand.

BILLY: I was thinking, locked up below there . . . the Captain knows the rights of all this. He'll save me if it's right. Then you sent for me. Is there hope for me, Captain?

VERE: Billy, what hope is there?

BILLY: Tell me why. I only want to understand.

VERE: How young you still are, Billy! Oh, I can tell you this: nothing is lost of anything that happens. I have given you the judgment of the world . . . deadly constraint . . . a length of hemp and a yardarm. I have done this to you, no one else.

BILLY: I can't get the rights of all that's happened.

VERE: There's not much right, Billy. Only necessity. You and

Claggart broke man's compromise with good and evil, and both of you must pay the penalty.

BILLY: Penalty? What for? Would anyone make laws just to be broken by fellows like me?

VERE: Aye, boy. You have learned this late. Most of us find out early and trim to a middle course.

BILLY: Do you mean . . . it's better to be like that?

VERE: Better as this world goes. When a man is born, he takes a guilt upon him, I can't say how or why. And life takes its revenge on those who hurt its pride with innocence.

BILLY: Do you think Claggart knew it would come to this?

VERE: He knew he would kill you, and he died to gain that end. But if you trust me, he'll not win entirely.

BILLY: How could he hate me like that?

VERE: The world we breathe is love and hatred both, but hatred must not win the victory.

BILLY: Claggart is dead. Now I'm to hang. Doesn't that show the law is wrong, when it can't choose between him and me?

VERE: Yes, it's all wrong, all wrong.

BILLY: I don't know, Captain. I never was a hand to wonder about things, but now I think that maybe there's a kind of cruelty in people that's just as much a part of them as kindness, say, or honesty, or m-m-m . . . I can't find words, I s'pose, Captain.

VERE: There are no words. We are all prisoners of deadly forms that are made to break us to their measure. Nothing has power to overcome them, except forgiveness . . . Can you forgive what I have done?

BILLY: I *can* trust you, can't I? *Can* you show me it's all right, my being . . .

VERE (*turns away; a long pause*): It's nearly dawn, lad. In the Spanish villages they're lighting fires.

BILLY: I'm not afraid, sir. (*Steps toward Vere.*) It's getting light.

VERE: There's no time for either of us left. Go, take the

morning. God knows you have the right to it. And when you are on the mainyard, think of me, and pray for those who must make choices. Hallam. (*Enter* HALLAM *in doorway.*) Take Budd into your charge. (BILLY *and* HALLAM *go out.*) Time has run out.

SCENE 3

Main deck aft. Drum-to-formation. Crew forming up. WYATT, *Midshipmen* GARDINER *and* REA.

WYATT: Bear a hand. Form the men up in ranks.

GARDINER: Aye, sir. All right, you! Close ranks! Move up, Stoll. That's better. Talbot, square your hat. Form up straight there, damn it! (*Drum.* MEN *come to attention.*)

WYATT: Division commanders report!

VOICE (*off*): Carpenters and gunners, present or accounted for, sir!

VOICE (*off*): Marine Detachment, present or accounted for, sir!

VOICE (*off*): Afterguard, present or accounted for, sir!

GARDINER: Fore, main and mizzentopmen . . . one absentee!

WYATT: All hands will stand by to witness punishment! Stand easy.

VOICES (*off*): Stand easy! (WYATT *walks away from men. Murmur in ranks.*)

KINCAID: Where the devil is Billy? He wasn't in his hammock when they piped us up.

O'DANIEL: He'll be getting himself in trouble if he don't fall in.

KINCAID: Who the hell they punishing, and what for?

JENKINS: It's got to be flogging, or they wouldn't have us all up here.

KINCAID: Vere never flogs anybody. And there ain't no gratings up.

THE DANSKER: They flog men at noon. The early morning's for hanging.

KINCAID: Hanging! (*The word travels back.*) Who? What for?

O'DANIEL: The skipper, he don't confide in me no more.

KINCAID: I thought they waited till they got ashore before they hanged a man.

THE DANSKER: Not in wartime.

JENKINS: He goes up them ratlines, out on the yard, they slips a noose around his neck, and then he jumps and hangs himself.

O'DANIEL: They'd have the devil's work getting O'Daniel to jump.

KINCAID: It's jump, or get pushed.

JENKINS: Where's Claggart? God, you don't suppose it's Claggart! Oh, Judas, let it be that fishblooded nark!

KINCAID: Not him. He's too smart, he is.

JENKINS: Where is he, then? He ain't here.

THE DANSKER: He is here.

KINCAID: Where? I don't see him.

THE DANSKER: He is here.

KINCAID: Ah . . . you're barmy, old man.

Enter VERE, SEYMOUR, RATCLIFFE *and the* SURGEON. *Drum sounds Attention.*

WYATT (*to Seymour*): Ship's company present to witness execution, sir.

SEYMOUR: Very well. (*To Vere.*) Ship's company present to witness execution, sir. (VERE *nods.*) (*To Wyatt.*) Lieutenant Wyatt, have the prisoner brought forward.

WYATT: Aye aye, sir. (*Marches to wing.*) Sentries, bring forward the prisoner. (*Marches back to his post.*)

Enter BILLY *with two sentries. Astonished murmur through the crew, who momentarily break ranks.*

WYATT: No talking in ranks! (*Continued restless movement and murmurings.*) Form up!

GARDINER: You men are at attention!

WYATT (*over subdued muttering*): You hear me? Silence in ranks!

Silence. SENTRIES *lead Billy to the foot of the ropes.* SEYMOUR *looks at* VERE, *who nods.* SEYMOUR *steps forward and reads.*

SEYMOUR: Proceedings of the court-martial held aboard H.M.S. *Indomitable* on the eighth of August, 1798. Convened under the authority of Edward Fairfax Vere, Senior Captain, Royal Navy, and composed of the First Officer, the Sailing Master, and the First Lieutenant of said vessel. In the case of William Budd, foretopman, Royal Navy. While attached and so serving in the aforesaid vessel, he did, on the eighth day of August, 1798, strike and kill his superior officer, one John Claggart, Master-at-Arms, Royal Navy.

Crew breaks out uneasily, astonished, talking excitedly.

JENKINS: Billy! Did you, boy?
VOICE: Good lad!
VOICE: Serves him proper!
KINCAID: Hi, Billy! Hurrah!

All together.

WYATT: Quiet! Silence, you men! Form up!

GARDINER: Stand at attention, hang you! Silence in the ranks!

WYATT: Do you hear? (*Excited muttering, low voices.*)

SEYMOUR: You will be silent and remain at strict attention until dismissed. (*Silence.*) . . . Master-at-Arms, Royal Navy. Therefore, the court sentences the aforementioned William Budd, foretopman, Royal Navy, to die by hanging on the first watch of the day following these proceedings. By authority of his Gracious Majesty George Rex and Alan Napier, Viscount Kelsey, First Sea Lord. Signed, Philip Seymour, Senior Member.

During the last phrases of the reading, the crew, upon hearing the sentence, breaks out again, some stepping forward, shouting; they are in an ugly temper.

VOICES: No he don't!
Not if I know it!
Hang the jemmies instead, I say!
Not Billy, you swineheads!
Not him, by God!
You ain't hanging Billy, damn your eyes!
Let them dance on a rope's end!
All together.

WYATT: Stand back! Sentries, guard your prisoner, if you have to fire!

GARDINER: Stand back, you damned clods! Keep back!

SEYMOUR (*steps forward*): Silence there! You will resume discipline instantly! Be warned. (*Waits a silent moment. Men stop in disordered formation.*) Stand back into ranks.

GARDINER: Form up again, quick about it now! (*There is a surly movement into irregular lines.*)

SEYMOUR (*warily resuming procedure*): Prisoner, have you anything to say? (BILLY *shakes his head.*) If you have nothing to say, when the drum roll is sounded, you will proceed to carry out the sentence of this court. (*Signals to Wyatt.*)

WYATT: Sound off.

Drum roll. BILLY *turns and starts up the ropes.*

VOICES: Get him! Now!
Bill! Stay where you are, boy, don't do it!
Wait, Billy! Wait!
Rush the deck, mates! Don't let them do it!
We're here, Bill, don't you worry!
All together.

BILLY (*stops, turns forward, looks at Vere, and shouts out loud and clear, without trace of stammer*): God bless Captain Vere!

A second's pause; VERE *is profoundly shaken;* BILLY *goes quickly up the ropes and out of sight. The crew moves back a step, is silent; officers and men in deep breathless quiet watch him out of sight and are staring overhead as the curtain falls.*

HISTORICAL NOTE

The background of the Mutinies of 1797 is very important to the action of *Billy Budd*. The first of these mutinies broke out in April among the Channel Fleet, lying at Spithead. The sailors refused to put to sea until they obtained fair wages, sufficient food of decent quality, better medical service and some shore leave at the end of a voyage. Faced with what was more a strike than a mutiny, the cabinet granted these demands within a week, and the fleet returned to duty, sailing to its station off Brest.

The mutiny of the North Sea Fleet at the Nore in May was a far more violent affair. 'It was indeed,' Melville wrote, 'a demonstration more menacing to England than the contemporary manifestoes and conquering and proselyting armies of the French Directory.' Melville was exaggerating, but the mutiny was a serious threat, particularly since it contained a sinister political element not present in the Spithead mutiny. Demands were made for a fairer division of prize money and for a modification of the brutal rules of discipline. Although few of the sailors appear to have agreed on the extent of their demands or on the lengths to which they were prepared to go, they threatened to blockade the Thames and it was only after they started fighting among themselves that the mutiny could be put down. This was done in July with considerable severity, and Richard Parker, the leader, was hanged. The speed with which the North Sea Fleet returned to normal is shown by the fact that it was only three months later that it destroyed the Dutch invasion fleet in the major battle of Camperdown.

Probably the Mutinies did have a considerable effect in producing more tolerable conditions in the Navy. Certainly they spotlighted the primitive conditions that existed at the time. In *Billy Budd* it is evident that 'Spithead' and 'The Nore' were already an awesome part of history. O'Daniel, for instance, has added status among his fellows because he had been 'at Spithead'. Claggart justifies his reporting of Billy to Vere by saying 'God forbid, sir, that this ship should suffer the experience of the Nore.' The mutinies provide a realistic and ever-present background to the action of the play.

A NAVAL NOTE

H.M.S. *Indomitable* is a Ship of the Line, i.e. a large ship designed to take her place in the line of battle in a major action against an enemy fleet. She has three masts: *fore*, *main* and *mizzen* and is 'square rigged', the principal sails going across the ship and being made fast to yards. The main sail on each mast is called the *course* and above that are *topsails*, *top gallants* (pronounced *t'gallants*) and *royals*. *Tops* are platforms on the masts.

The Ship's Company is organized in Divisions, three of which are called after the parts of the ship where the men's duty lies. Hence the terms *foretopman* or *Captain of the Main Top*.

Time is indicated by the striking of a bell every half-hour up to the number of eight which ends the four-hour watch. The notes are struck in pairs with a short pause after each pair.

The *Master at Arms* is the senior man on board below the rank of Officer. A *Midshipman* is a subordinate Officer, and an *Admiralty Midshipman* is one appointed to the ship by the Admiralty instead of being appointed by the Captain as was then the more usual custom.

GLOSSARY

Abeam, 33: At right angles to the ship
Afterguardsmen, 17: A division of the crew
Articles of War, 13: The code which regulated discipline in the Navy. Originally, the Articles of War were regulations issued by the king to govern the conduct of the forces during a war, and they would cease to operate at the end of the war. After the Jacobite rebellion of 1715, however, the Mutiny Act (see separate note) authorized the king to issue Articles of War during peacetime, too. It is under the Articles of War that Vere is able to summon the special drumhead court-martial. The Articles of War have now been embodied in the Naval Discipline Act, a permanent statute, first passed in 1866
Bargemen, 7: Weevils, a type of maggot found in ship's biscuits. Thus, O'Daniel is saying that the weevils that are in the Navy biscuits would be big enough to eat the Captain's bird
Beat-to-Quarters, 23: The beat of a drum used to summon the Ship's Company to action stations
Belay it, 10: Stop it. From belaying a rope, which is to secure it in order to stop it running out
Belay your mess gear, 11: Tidy up your equipment
Between decks, 9: The decks below the upper decks. The point here is that the Master-at-Arms would not be under the observation of the Officers
Bill, 36: The list of the men's duties
Bole, 36: Trunk (as of a tree, but here, of the mast)
Braces, 34: The ropes used to alter the direction of the yards
Captain, 14: It is highly unlikely that either the Officers or the men would have addressed Vere as 'Captain'. It would have been correct to have addressed him as 'Captain Vere', but the most usual form would have been simply 'Sir'
Cat, 26: Short for the *cat-o-nine-tails*, the instrument used for flogging. It was made of rope and had nine tails
Close-hauled, 31: Sailing as close as possible to the direction from which the wind is coming

Companionway, 1, 5, 13: Ladder

Compartment, 1, 2, 4, 13: A divided-off space between decks

Cover and Uncover, 17: Put on, take off caps.

Cullion, 4: Wretch, rascal

Dissynchronously, 30: The distinction here is that, instead of firing in unison, the guns are fired as soon as they are reloaded

Drumhead, 47: A Court-Martial convened without the normal formalities

Eyes in the boat, 5: 'Eyes front' primarily, thus to mind one's behaviour. Derived from the rule that the crew of a rowing boat are supposed to look aft

Fathom, 28: A measurement of the depth of water equal to six feet

First Officer, xii: In fact there was no such rank as First Officer in the Navy and the senior person under the Captain was First Lieutenant. There was a rank of Master, this Officer being especially in charge of the navigation. Readers may be interested to know that, before the Navy properly existed (which may be said to be before Henry VIII established a Naval Board, under the direction of a Lord High Admiral) the Captain and the Lieutenant were military men who came on board a Merchant Ship to do the fighting, while the Master and his Mates were the permanent Sea Officers of the ship

Flukes, 28: The points of an anchor

Footpad, 27: A robber who pursued his calling on foot as distinguished from the highwayman who used a horse

Forechains, 41: *The chains* were platforms on the ship's side where the leadsman stood to measure the depth of water with a lead and line. The lee forechains suited Claggart's purpose because they were secluded

Forefoot, 36: The slim part of a ship's hull on either side of the bows

Glass, 22: Barometer

Grating, 3, 67: A wooden platform. Men were lashed to an upended grating to be flogged

Guano, 8: The dung of sea-fowl, and therefore a coarse exclamation

Halyards, 34: Ropes used to hoist the yards

Hatchway, 12, 13: The opening in the deck through which one reaches the *Companionway* to the deck below.

Haul in the slops, 2: Bring in the food
His Majesty's bounty, 7: Rations
Hitch, 8: Period of Service
Hooker, 8: Originally a type of sailing ship and generally as a term of affectionate contempt
Hove down, 23: Pulled down and thus lying low
Jemmies, 70: Ship's police
Larboard, 5: (Nowadays called port.) The left hand side of a ship looking towards the bow. The right hand side is the starboard
Lay aloft, 25: Go aloft
Leeward, 20: See *Windward*
Levanter, 32: A boisterous easterly wind in the Levant (the East)
Lobcock, 32: A clumsy person, a lout
Lobscouse, 7: A stew with preserved vegetables or biscuit
Manacles, 64: Handcuffs
Manta, 12: A type of gigantic fish, like a ray
Mess, 6: The living space of a number of men who share a *mess table* (1) and *messboy* (3, 12) – a junior rating whose job it is to clean up the mess and fetch food
Mutiny Act, 56: The Act of Parliament which gave the king his forces and laid down how they were to be run: the Articles of War became incorporated as part of the Act in 1715
Nore, 45: The scene of one of the Naval Mutinies of 1797 (see historical note)
Pleach, 36: An intertwining of ropes
Prating, 20: Prattling, talking foolishly
Pressed, 2, 6, 8, 14: i.e. Impressed. Compelled to serve in the Navy without having volunteered to do so. Men could be impressed from British Merchant Ships as well as on shore in Britain. Impressment had been regularized by Act of Parliament in 1795. Those impressed were to be able-bodied men between the ages of 16 and 50, who were unable to 'prove themselves to exercise and industriously follow some lawful Trade or Employment'. The press-gang was, however, notorious for its methods, and the new Act probably took effect only very slowly.
Put us to our stations, 22: Cause us to take up our positions for fighting
Quarterdeck, 17, 31: The aftermost deck, at a higher level than the main

deck. The break of the quarter deck is where it ends and the level descends to the main deck

Quartermaster, 30: The man whose duty it was to take the wheel and steer the ship under the instruction of the Officer of the Watch

Ratlines, 17: The masts are supported on each side by a row of stout ropes called shrouds which run from the ship's side near to the top of the main mast. The ratlines are smaller ropes secured to the shrouds like the steps of a ladder up which men climb to go aloft

Rattan, 12: A cane

Reef sail, 31: To reduce the area of the sail. This is done by tying up the bottom of the sail with reef points which are small lines fitted to the sail

Sound off, 29: In dialogue 'State name and rank'. As stage direction 'Beat-to-quarters'

Spar-deck, 40: The part of the upper deck where the spars (i.e. spare yards, etc.) were kept

Spithead, 4, 9: The scene of one of the Naval Mutinies of 1797

Squared away, 5: Organized

Square your hat, 67: Put your hat at the right angle

String him to a yard, 57: Hang him

Stripes, 58: The reference to 'gold stripes across our arms' is an anachronism. Although the French were adopting stripes to indicate the rank of non-commissioned officers at about this time, the practice was not copied by the British forces until quite a few years later. It is interesting to note that, in Melville's novel, Vere says 'do these buttons that we wear attest that our allegiance is to Nature?' He is simply referring to the fact that they are wearing the uniforms of His Majesty's Navy, which would have had gold buttons at the front and the cuffs

Trim to a middle course, 65: Go neither to one extreme or another

Turn topside, 2: Go up on deck

Windward and Leeward: Windward, 23: The side of the ship from which the wind is coming; *Leeward*, 20: (pronounced *Looard*) the opposite side

Work to windward, 23: To try and get the better of something

Yardarm, 14, 49: The outer end of a yard